*Under the Tongue*

In *Under the Tongue* Vera's style is beautifully matched with the content, and magnificently promotes its central theme that language has both the power to heal and to accrete and to allow those who have once been victims to transform themselves and their future. (Judges citation: Commonwealth Writer's Prize: Africa Region)

*Under the Tongue* cements Vera's place as a pre-eminent African novelist. By tackling the subjects of incest and child-abuse, Vera challenges the silence with which these issues are met in our society. *The National News.*

*Under the Tongue* is told in mesmerizing detail, as we are led into the agonizing depths of violence and despair. *The Herald.*

*Under the Tongue* is about suffering [and] it is also about speaking out. More specifically it is about women speaking out. That is the gift that Zhiza offers, not just to her silent mother and her remembering grandmother not just to the doubly oppressed women of Zimbabwe ... but to women all over the world. *The Zimbabwe Review.*

In Vera, Zimbabwe has at last found its only too disturbing and plangent chronicler and critic. *Weekly Mail and Guardian.*

# Under the Tongue

Yvonne Vera

Published by Baobab Books, P.O. Box 567, Harare
A division of Academic Books (Pvt) Ltd, Harare

First published 1996, reprinted 1997

Published in South Africa by David Philip Publishers (Pty) Ltd
208 Werdmuller Centre, Claremont 7700

*Photograph of Yvonne Vera by:* Godfrey Moyo
*Cover design:* Mary Clare Foa
*Typeset by:* Baobab Books
*Printed by:* Mazongororo Paper Converters (Pvt.) Ltd.

The author would like to express her appreciation to the Ontario Arts
Council and the Canada Council for the arts awards granted to her in
1995 which enabled her to have time to write.

BAOBAB BOOKS

ISBN 0-908311-93-1

ISBN 0-86486-353-5

Yvonne Vera was born in Bulawayo, Zimbabwe, where she now lives. Her collection of short stories *Why Don't You Carve Other Animals,* and her novels *Nehanda* and *Without a Name* were short-listed in the Commonwealth Writer's Prize for 1993, 1994 and 1995 respectively. *Without a Name* won her the Zimbabwe Publisher's Literary Award. *Under the Tongue* won the Commowealth Writers Prize (Africa region) in 1997, and was awarded first prize in the 1997 Zimbabwe Book Publisher's Literary Awards.

Yvonne Vera is a doctoral graduate of York University, Toronto. She is now the Director of the National Gallery of Zimbabwe in Bulawayo.

### For Lilian B. Mboyi

*Courage,*
*friendship,*
*love, these three.*
*After that,*
*we are as burnt as ash,*
*and lighter still.*

# 1

*A* tongue which no longer lives, no longer weeps. It is buried beneath rock.

My tongue is a river. I touch my tongue in search of the places of my growing. My tongue is heavy with sleep. I know a stone is buried in my mouth, carried under my tongue. My voice has forgotten me. Only Grandmother's voice remembers me. Her voice says that before I learnt to forget there was a river in my mouth.

She cries about the many tongues which lie in the mouth, withered, without strength to speak the memory of their forgetting. Such tongues do not bleed. They have abandoned the things of life.

I listen. A murmur grows into my awakening, from Grandmother. She wipes her forehead with her hand and her voice embraces all my fear. She leans forward with arms held tightly over her shoulders. Then she brings her arms like a gift toward me, and she pulls a root which has grown deep inside her chest. Her eyes pull this root from inside her and I watch her lips tremble, her arms so silent, her voice departed, her elbows bare. She pulls this root from her mouth, from beneath her tongue. I know that this root begins inside me and that Grandmother will find where it begins. I know she placed it there before I was born, before my mother was born. She bends forward, once more, her arms folded and she waits, shivering with release. I know that her waiting is also her giving.

Her voice says we can touch the sky even if it is so far away. We cannot fear our silence, our desire, our release. When our voices reach the sky with their crying, rain will fall and cover the earth. The sky will become a river, Grandmother says.

Rivers begin in the sky. Rivers begin with our tears. Grandmother's cry follows me everywhere. I touch my tongue. It is heavy like stone. I do not speak. I know nothing of rivers. Grandmother is a river. I am not Grandmother. My arms spread over her shoulders and I rest my face along her face. I listen to her voice roll over her back, tumbling, and I laugh. Grandmother is a river. The river is inside her body. The river is held in her mouth, held in her body.

Grandmother will be carried by the river which waits inside her, waits to be remembered. I know if I do not enter the river I will never find her again. I listen to her cry which carries all my sorrow of yesterday and I know that I have brought this river to her. I am inside Grandmother. I am Grandmother.

It is not true that rivers come from the sky, she says.

I do not fear the darkness. Grandmother protects me with her weeping, tells me of the many places, the many sorrows, the many wounds women endure. She tells me about herself, about my mother Runyararo. Muroyiwa was the name of my father. Grandmother tells me about night, about my father. Muroyiwa. My father. This darkness is heavy as stone. Grandmother will teach me many forgotten songs.

She sings a lament. Not for silence, not for death.

***

A voice scrambles, turns into night.

Zhizha.

Father whispers an embrace of lightning. I bite hard on my tongue, hold my breath deep in my chest. My voice is sinking down into my stomach. My voice is crumbling and falling apart and spreading through his fingers. My voice hides beneath rock. My voice burns beneath my chest. Lightning finds me, embraces the moon, finds me fallen from the sky. I hear father.

Zhizha.

Singing . . .

Zhizha do not cry water is sleep not death.

But my voice is lost. Astray. Salt spreads through my eyes. My eyes are dry like stone. My voice blinded. My voice wishing to escape. My voice pulled from its roots, dug from sleep. My voice falling. My voice empty and forgotten. My voice slips in a dying whirl that grows small and faint. My cry is stolen.

I hear crushing in my stomach. Water pulling at my dream, pulling at rock, pulling at my sleep. I awaken. An embrace, once more, of lightning, entering my sleep.

A burning grows deep beneath the sky. A shadow grows on my chest, struggles to depart. I die in my sleep. My voice is held by the lingering shadow. I cannot speak. I lie inside stone.

Then a soundless cry, still and quiet . . .

sh sh sh

Father speaks in an unremembered voice. He has swallowed sleep. I see father waiting in my sleep. I see father in the midst of my cry. I see father. Father . . .

Zhizha.

He calls in a whisper and cry. Father . . . His voice is full of the unknown things of my growing destroying sleep. His voice says death is also life. He calls my name in the midst of night. Father . . . His whisper is heavier than night, than dream, than silence. He carries death in his arms, banishes morning.

Father holds my breathing in his palm. His palm is wide and widening, grooved and wet. Then he lifts a heavy arm and touches the edge of the moon, in my sleep. I shout through fingers so strong, so hard, his fingers saying in their buried touch

Zhizha . . . Zhizha.

A hidden visit.

I cry but my cry meets silence. My voice has lost the promises of day. I hear my voice fall like a torrent down into my stomach. My voice meets rock, meets water, grows silent and dead. Father calls in my sleep. My voice grows still, and waits in a trembling quiet. I turn my face away and run from the moon. I listen. The moon banishes sleep and dream.

A shadow grows from the moon. The shadow lifts me from the ground. I wait beneath a fervent sky. The shadow of the moon has turned bright with the serenity of death. The moon is wounded by the darkness.

I search for the moon which has left the sky. Memory has left the sky. It is night.

. . . Zhizha.

I see a scar grow farther and farther. I am certain this is the path through which I will be born. The scar widens, peels like bark. I wait.

Father . . .

I do not want to see father, ever.

Your father has died, Grandmother says.

I turn away, sleep falling through my eyelids. Grandmother places a warm hand over my forehead.

Father has drunk the forbidden water from the sea, swallowed the deep unknown things of my growing, swallowed night. I see father, his forehead bruised. I heard him fall yesterday crushing like rock. He turns to me in the salt dark of the sea, saying,

Zhizha these are the secrets of the sea.

He reaches a cold hand toward me but I stand in sunlight, calling for my mother. I wait and wait. I have forgotten the song of my growing. I long to hear the name of my mother. I long to defeat the silence. I listen beyond the pounding of my heart, the pleading voice of my grandmother.

Zhizha.

Father died in his sleep, in his dreaming. I reach a trembling hand across his forehead. He breathes hard, saying

these are the secrets of the sea.

No, in my dreaming. My hands held tight, my fingers crushed, my bones broken dry like rock so broken. I see Grandmother, a harvest of weeds covering her arms. Grandmother, embracing my cry. Father drowned while he slept.

The sky gathers both earth and cloud. The sky meets the river moving beneath stone. The river rises. Father pulls me down into the river.

He pulls at my dream and I sink beneath the pounding which falls through my eyes.

It is night.

Roots grow out of my stomach out of my mouth out of me. My cry is silence. My cry searches the river, wavers between bending reeds, finds father waiting and near. He holds my hand. He pulls hard at my arm. He pulls the roots in my growing, the dream in my belonging. I cry in a voiceless tremble, my eyes parched with darkness.

I close my eyes and do not speak. My mouth is covered with blood.

I call for mother but Grandmother says . . . do not be afraid Grandmother is here. I close my eyes and find a lullaby in my sleep.

I find Grandmother.

In my sleep.

## 2

It was during the war that Muroyiwa looked for butterflies in the mountains. He had travelled a long way to the mountains to find them. When he arrived there he wondered what happened to the butterflies during a war.

His birth haunted him while he permitted himself to live. Permission, willed and visible, this living, because often he had to pause and think about his mother, being born, about the calabash. When next he died, it would be because he had succumbed to the will of another.

His mother spoke of retrieving him from a calabash. Muroyiwa failed to make tangible the distinction between any two emotions so he pretended the confusion did not matter. He did think about it briefly between one breath and the next, and that was not time at all. When he thought deeply about it, he felt like an insect thrown defencelessly against the earth, not camouflaged against the task of being so constantly threatened with living.

An insect. How else could his mother have managed to retrieve him, limbs, arms, head and toes, from a calabash, if he had not been an insect. The calabashes he had seen were small. He could not imagine being retrieved from any one of them. Now that he was a man he could not comfortably think of being born in a calabash, but his mother said this had happened, and another further miracle, he had died at birth then awakened the following morning, so they named him Muroyiwa. The lulling ease with which his mother said he had awakened made death seem similar to sleep, simply a wave of calm, not the tumult of agony which the war married with death.

Folded into a calabash, ready for the burial which would occur in the early morning, but Muroyiwa rose too with the morning. Afterwards the women could not bury him. They were not joyous either; they preferred him not to live. This was clear throughout his early life. To absolve everyone of any malice in wishing him death, Muroyiwa quickly assumed that death was better than life, more to be wished for. It was this which made living tolerable, the constancy of death. Life tantalized him with its promises of an ultimate and reachable fulfillment. Someone had to be blamed other than himself for that struggle out of the calabash. It was appropriate to say that he had been bewitched.

Muroyiwa had gathered death from inside a calabash and reduced it to a shade of sleep. Such a light thing, this death, sweet, pulsating with the eternity of sleep. When he first understood the meaning of his name Muroyiwa could no longer escape from life. This he considered during the war when he allowed himself to be haunted by beauty and loving and the symmetry of mats, then he forgot about the war, or at least he fought its encroachment. The war made him see clearly the objects he wanted to see. It was like seeing thunder when the sky is black with rain. Muroyiwa was not blind to lightning, its tantalizing beauties.

War was black like the sky; beauty purified war. Then a desperate passion engaged him and would not let him free. Muroyiwa carried a calabash inside him, where his heart should have been and there were no cobwebs of death in it, only an untarnished desire for living. He discovered the anxiety of death licked with the waiting that accompanied war. It was the waiting he fought against more than the war itself. He conceived a strategy to fight against waiting. This came in the pursuit of a limitless charm, of living. When he thought further on this desire he saw that such charm would not be found simply anywhere, but would be embodied in a form, perhaps that of a woman.

Muroyiwa became anxious. This anxiety of death unlike other visitations, he understood without remorse.

A lack of remorse is not happiness, it is freedom from the anxiety of living.

≈≈≈≈≈≈

# 3

$\mathcal{M}$y eyelids collapse, heavy with sleep.

I hear voices filled with tears. Darkness trembles with the memory of the moon. It is night.

Grandmother cries for our origins. We met in water, she cries. Our dreams are birth and death.

In the gathering darkness Grandmother's voice rises piercing into the night, is swallowed by the darkness, returns in one tremulous echo, rises again surging forward, tumbling in a cascade bright with moon seeking the forgotten, the departed, who wait to be remembered.

We wait for healing mysteries to visit us. The horizon ripens a golden brightness growing in a splendid growth so rare. It is morning. I hear Grandmother sing a song about the sorrows of the world, the grief of yesterday which follows her. She sings about finding a memory in her dreams, a memory that will be for healing not sorrow. She sings about one large moon so large it carries many moons in it, hangs low as though it will touch the earth. Grandmother will harvest the milk of the moon for Mother, for me. We wait.

I have searched the sky, Grandmother sings. It sits on my forehead, this moon. Grandmother says it is sometimes good to forget, to bury the heavy things of now, the things which cannot be remembered without death becoming better than life. Such things are for forgetting, for burying beneath the earth. But a woman must remember the moment of birth and of death.

*\*\**

I hear my cry carried in Grandmother's mouth. She has found me. I am Grandmother. Grandmother cries for me and for my mother. She buries all our sorrows in her crying. Her cry swallows everything, swallows our fears.

Grandmother says we choose words, not silence. We choose words to bury our grief. A woman cannot say the heaviness of her life, just like that, without madness. A woman must speak the beauties and the sorrows of the heart, she must dream a celebration. A woman must not forget, she must not bury her sorrow and her dreams. If a woman buries her sorrow, a dream will kill her children. A woman sings the wisdom of her heart, sings her waiting, greets the moment of birth, defeats death and silence. Tonderayi, Grandmother cries about the forgotten whose sorrow has been awakened.

We met in water, Grandmother cries into mother's growing silence.

Grandmother cries to the stars and the shadows and the mysteries of the earth. She says I am part of her, that she is birth and dawn, she is mother. It is warm, she says. It is very painful but warm, over your legs, like waves. Birth is like water turning gently into cloud. We cannot hide our tears when sorrow has visited us like this, she says, our tears are as old as the daughters and mothers and grandmothers of our ancient earth, dear as birth, like morning and dew. These tears, they are warm like the earth, do not forget. We cry for birth and long to see ourselves in water. We seek our peace from the beginning of our being, from the mouth of rivers, from mothers. A daughter is the birth of dream, a daughter is daylight on growing leaves. Daughters are our mothers, Grandmother says. She carries my pain in her mouth. I know Grandmother will heal me with her word, her word that is for remembering all that has visited her suffering, that has accompanied my growing. Tonderayi . . . again she laments with all the moments of our birth.

Grandmother calls to me and to mother, Mother-of-Zhizha, she calls to my mother. Birth is the remembering of journeying, it is not to be forgotten. We are women. We belong together in an ancient caress of the earth. We are full of giving like the parting of clouds, gently falling, carrying the promises of growth, of a season serene with maturation.

Zhizha, Grandmother pleads.

It is night and Grandmother turns into an unforgettable whisper of lament. She throws our voices to the moon. She gives us a song for healing, for a memory without sorrow. The song buries all our desperation and our loss. Her voice rises and the moon grows bright into our dreaming, moving and turning a trembling light, round and smooth with her weariless giving. She throws our voices to the sky and night falls around our faces, feathery over our outstretched arms. The moon grows wide into the sky with Grandmother's calling, growing wide. The moon covers the sky.

Grandmother throws our voices to the moon. There are no stars in the sky only our voices. The woman on the moon is bearing a load on her head. She has travelled through the sky. She has seen all the pain of the world.

Grandmother's voice vanishes into the darkness. We wait. Her voice turns to a whisper thin with our desires. We wait for the unpredictable wonders that will beautify our dreams. We wait for morning. In our waiting a memory awakens our voices. Grandmother weeps. Her tears are darkness and dream. I will follow the shadow of the moon, Grandmother says of her pain. She calls, holding our dream between her fingers, fingers that are tender roots of fond longing. We witness the creeping of dew, on grass, in her dreaming.

It is morning. We remember the moon which has swallowed our voices.

We long to forget the thunder of departing innocence.

The sound tells me she has died.

I wait for the sound to tell me again that Grandmother has died.

I wait, afraid to move my feet, to breathe, move my arms, but the sound vanishes and refuses to return. I know that the sound accompanies her secret and her living and it is not to be forgotten. I turn my head rapidly to my left. I look again for the slow sound. My eyes search on the floor, everywhere. I search for Grandmother. When I find her she is resting still where I wait. I stand near. I stand near to myself. I see my legs, my feet, near Grandmother. I lift my arms and allow the air, thick, tainted with burning wood to move through me.

I am sure the heavy things of the world have entered Grandmother and defeated her, made her fall. She is so still it makes me tremble hard and fearful because I can hear again the slow heavy sound. The sound is behind my head, somewhere near, behind my ears. I dare not turn. I tremble till my trembling is quiet. I hate the quiet. It tastes like warm salt, on my lips.

Something moves between me and Grandmother and falls a great fall reaching my feet and slides between my toes. I hear the drops over my feet. I do not move. I watch my toes dissolve. I watch my feet which are no longer my feet. They are large, not quite there, not part of me. It is the same with my arms which have discovered their own ability for silence. Only my shoulders say these are my arms.

I raise my head up from the ground and from my feet, very carefully, and find the roof which seems so far away. My eyes fill with patches of soot. I search the wall's deep black, clotted with smoke. A flat winnowing basket is suspended against the wall. A frayed rope, once white, dangles over the basket and swings softly upward when I look. Behind the basket is the grey tail of a lizard. The tail is large and points downward, almost dead, like the rope. I wish grandfather would come home before I am swallowed by the things which have grown between me and Grandmother. Grown and grown.

I hide somewhere behind my eyes. I remember. I hide deep inside my head. Her falling like this has something to do with me, with my mother. I have brought this death to Grandmother.

Grandmother opens her eyes and asks for my name. I am quiet wondering if she thinks I am my mother. Runyararo, I say. A woman always remembers her child, Grandmother has told me. I am not Grandmother's child. She has remembered her child, my mother, not me. Runyararo . . . I say very loud.

The name falls and follows Grandmother to the ground and lies still. Runyararo . . . I do not understand why the name has followed Grandmother like that, followed us. I look for the name on the ground but I cannot move my arms. I cannot find the name with my arms. I do not move. The name lies still on my lips, watered with tears.

Runyararo . . . I carry the name in my mouth once more. It falls again. Runyararo . . . I search the ground through my tears. Runyararo . . . I see Grandmother. Runyararo . . . She closes her eyes again and sleeps. Her sleep has taken her and hidden her far where I cannot find her. I am afraid. I stand very far from Grandmother. I stand outside Grandmother, outside myself. I see mother. My mother not me my mother. Runyararo . . . I must give the name to Grandmother not mother. Runyararo . . . This is her name of birth and I must return the name to

13

her where she can find it. I give Grandmother the name bathed with loneliness and longing. Runyararo. This word will heal Grandmother.

I remember the darkness and the night which have visited. I have to remember because the darkness has something to do with Grandmother being on the ground like this. Something helpless. The darkness has no shape or sound, just falling and dying and never getting up, like Grandmother. I know the darkness is just inside my head, somehow, waiting. It is not even inside my head. The inside of my head is not blue like morning though when I remember a blue like that it presses hard on my forehead and makes me cry. The inside of my head is wide. I know this from the pounding on both sides of my head. The inside of my head has swallowed darkness. Perhaps it is the sky which has entered me because sometimes I can see the morning rolled inside my head.

Grandmother says the sky is only words. The sky is inside us. The sky is hard to store in a small place even if it is only a word. The sky is water. Words are water too. I do not drown in the sky. Drowning is death. Grandmother says those buried in the ground have also drowned. A soft drowning of words. How can we be buried when no words have been uttered. Only words can bury us, she says. How can death arrive when the mouth has not allowed it to arrive. Death has a name which we can carry in the mouth without dying. Only words can bury us not silence.

In the darkness I see just one red dot and I can store it anywhere inside my head, even under my eye. I watch it move inside my head till it disappears. It grows very small. When I look at a small red dot it grows and fills my head. The darkness is very large. I am frightened. I hear Grandmother falling, dying. Runyararo . . .

Grandmother asks for my name again and I know she wants my real name not the name of my mother. Not mother, just me. My name not that of my mother. Grandmother says a woman's name is the one she has given to her child. Mother's name is me. Runyararo is the name of my grandmother because she gave the name to my mother. Mother carries Grandmother's name for her. I am mother.

Zhizha, I say. That is also my mother. I am mother. She is Grandmother. Zhizha is the soft fall of rain after harvest, a peaceful rain which is not for growing things but for mercy. It is a solemn kind of rain, lonely, with no song to it, just rain on brown leaves. Zhizha.

Harvest is green like birth. If crop is not harvested it turns brown and dies. Water will not give it life. Runyararo . . .

The name falls in drops on my tongue like rain in late harvest. I give Grandmother the word which I have wrapped in leaves which are almost dead. I fold the secret into the shaking palm of her hand where my life begins, and she guards it with her tongue.

I ask Grandmother why she has fallen like that and she says she has forgotten where she was going, where she is, the places of her wisdom. My arms are empty, she says. My arms do not remember what they were carrying. She opens her arms and looks slowly downward to the ground as though she will recover something fallen there, as though she will pick a dream from the ground and place it back in her arms, nestle it where it has fallen from, in the warm crevices of her arms.

Grandmother asks me to tell her about the emptiness in her arms but I do not know how to begin. She wants to know how her arms found this emptiness because this emptiness is too heavy for her to carry, much too heavy for her arms. It is the emptiness which found her. Her arms would never betray her like this, she says, finding an abandon so rare and shattering that her mouth refuses to name it. Grandmother searches deep into her arms. There is nothing in her arms but her eyes searching through that nothing which grows with her every searching, with her every pleading, nothing at all but her empty arms.

I want to tell Grandmother about the slow sound of her dying but the nothing in her arms defeats everything. Only the basket on the wall is waiting perhaps with words to be shelled and tossed, waiting with words to be chosen, cast aside, separated, dismissed. I look at the basket and know that the best words are those that are shared and embraced, those that give birth to other words more fruitful than themselves, stronger than themselves.

Grandmother. Her eyes have swallowed the emptiness that has filled her arms. Her eyes brim with the same abundant nothing which has filled her arms and made her fall, which has broken her knees and made her into a child. Grandmother says she walked into a void, an emptiness so surprising her shoulders were thoroughly unprepared for it.

I move my feet toward the tarnished wall and reach for the basket. The basket is far above my head but the rope is nearer so I pull hard at the rope which holds the basket to the wall and the basket falls into my waiting arms. There is a basket in my arms. I carry the basket across the silent room. I notice that my feet are my feet and I have also found my arms. I give the basket to Grandmother. I place it safely under her embrace. She touches my arms with a hopeful caress.

She moves her right hand inside the basket to gather something she has recently discovered, something that she has lost while gathering words.

≈≈≈≈≈≈

# 4

*I*f there were any butterflies in the mountains, Muroyiwa would meet their delicate caress like a restored blindness. He was curious to meet butterflies amid the sound of death, the wailing voices of women, the distresses of children, the dry desperation.

VaGomba was blind. Muroyiwa had been born into his father's blindness and it received and contained him like a vessel. At birth, he had moved from the calabash into the blindness and because of this for him the butterflies surrounding the mountains would be pitched louder than the sound of death. He had received many longings from his father's blindness. There was death in the mountains.

VaGomba. One morning a root had sprung from the earth and torn the sight from his eyes. He had been digging, preparing the fields for planting. Nearby was a large harmless stump. His hoe hit a root which sprung from the earth and hit him across the forehead, twice, across his eyes, like an angry whip. The whip was like trembling lightning. Unforgettable, merciless, the white root flashed a solid sound, then a sudden tearing gurgle filled the earth like a river before VaGomba fell into a sightless world. VaGomba, his face lacerated, curled his arms and rested them vigilantly over his eyes as though to protect them from a searing sun, lay still till the ground beneath stopped beating, his arms frilled with blood, his temples bursting. Past noon, the shadows long, tense, pulling fiercely into the trees. In these taut rhythms they left the fields.

Before they left VaGomba's wife Muroyiwa's mother, VaMirika, picked the discarded hoe and covered both portions of the split root hastily, furtively covered the blood which lay in dots scattered over the proud whiteness which was thick and bulging, buried the glossy root which was soft and slippery and harmless to her memory.

VaMirika went to her husband and tried to heal him. With her memory she again buried the deceptive root and its stealthy promises, levelled the ground with her foot, as though she no longer wished to touch the earth. She welcomed the ground's anonymity, its ability to forget tragedy no matter how bright with the colour of surprise.

She could not bury VaGomba's sorrow as easily, however, his shimmering anger which made the day's shadows the longest of that planting season, the heaviest, carrying all the heaviness of their shoulders. VaGomba gently refused her hand and found the path leading home, on his own. He groped with his bare feet till he found the path worn to thinness, with its welcoming thorns and the undulating morning laughters they had left in the early dew. The laughter had grown coarse, their voices brittle and dry like crushed seeds.

VaGomba never spoke of this incident except he said that something truly tight had risen from the earth and unbound him, separated him from himself. "From now on I will only see my shadow and the shadow of everything that surrounds us." He remembered – the shapes of things held in the hand, of pain held once across the eyes, recalled especially the feeling of that death. VaGomba found the shape of the absence of light; light travelling through water, on motionless lakes and rivers, and there was a sound to that light, through winds and the sound of that, light in the smoke above huts, and there was a sound too to that. In his mind the voicelessness of a single feather falling through light, meeting light wrapped upon a single grain of sand, moving above a yellow shoot of maize which has become a breath of fertile tenderness released kindly from the earth. The shape of the absence of light.

≈≈≈≈≈≈≈

# 5

$\mathcal{A}$ knife moves sharply on rock. I hear a cry like falling water, then silence.

I call in the night . . . Mother . . . Mother.

A knife moves sharply, over rock.

Mother . . .

I turn in my sleep. I listen. There is silence. A sound comes toward me. Thud, on the ground, at my feet. I run far into the night but I fall hard on the ground. Roots cover the ground, growing in knots, tightening, beyond my dream, into the morning. My legs and arms are caught in the the ground pulling me down into a lake deep and dark under the tree. I turn and turn but my feet are buried beneath the earth. I pull hard but the roots grow from my stomach and pull at my sleep. Water everywhere. Water and night. I sink, beneath dream. Thud. I wake from sleep. Then I turn again, and sleep. Nothing. My arms reach into the dark and search the silence. Nothing. Nothing but the fear growing across my forehead and blinding me. Night. Nothing but the soft night filled with the sound of dying dream, with my fingers, with my cry searching blindly. Thud. The sound moves upward and swallows the night. It dies slowly, in drops. My voice crawls out of my mouth and hangs somewhere beside that dying sound. The sound is me and I rise up to meet the darkness but the night is too heavy for my forehead and my arms. Something is held safely in my fingers, within the roots so many. I raise my feet from the ground, lift, shift, twist my arms. I pull my legs from the ground.

Roots grow from my knee, from my scar. I fold my knee and cover it with my hand and bury the secrets of my growing. The roots grow from deep inside my leg, from my bones. My scar grows wide. I listen to roots breaking softly in my bones. I listen to the softness in the silence. I remember my scar.

I hear a knife, moving sharply, over rock. A memory bursts from the sky, explodes in sharp piercing rays, burning, like flame. I run, my mouth covered in silence. I hear again the knife in the dark. I see mother. Mother. A door closes. Hard. The knife moves sharply again, on rock. A door opens and closes.

I hide under my tongue. I hide deep in the dark inside of myself where no one has visited where it is warm like blood. Night waits for my cry but I can only think of my knee bending slowly, painfully, touching the something, the nothing rising above my head, rising from my arms. I know this nothing is something, someone. I hear the door close. I do not want to think about this nothing which my arms remember, which has spread itself inside me, this something which hides. I fold my hand over my knee grown ripe with new wounds.

I run deep into the water my legs thick and heavy. I run. I fall. I fall a great height. I fall and fall and my voice meets me in collapsing waves, of sleep. My head is heavy because I have swallowed the water. My head grows and grows into my eyes. I have swallowed the gentle voice of my grandmother which pulls me from the river and I sleep a quiet sleep.

Grandmother is singing in the river. She sings about rivers which fold into the evening sky then vanish. She sings about the river which grows from beneath the hills where she has buried her memory. I follow her song into the hills where the air is deep and red and glowing and the sky is burning on our feet and tomorrow cannot be named. In the distance the hills embrace the sky in a horizon of slippery rays. The river grows from the sky.

I run because my voice is no longer me and my eyes are so filled with water. I run because my voice has fallen into a calabash inside my head. I wake inside a calabash where silence has no beginning, only death. Grandmother carries the calabash on her head and weeps. The river has followed Grandmother. She has brought the secrets of death in her mouth. I wait inside the river which Grandmother says begins in the mouth, begins inside the calabash, inside my tongue.

I hear a surging, violent, falling a thick cascade burying my song, in dawn and remembrance. I look for the joy in my growing. I long for tomorrow and daylight. I long for morning. I cry for Grandmother and she spreads her voice around me in a promise of birth. Her voice rises from her arms, like smoke, and I see the river which has watered our pain, which sings about all our belonging. A river is a mouth with which to begin.

It is morning. I find mother in my dream and I hear a knife, moving sharply, over rock.

Father . . .

\*\*\*

Lemon trees. The trees are taller than the houses. Mornings and evenings are bright with lemons, a vivid yellow, a vibrant hue over the rooftops.

Our house is small, three tight rooms. On a silent hot afternoon a loud sound like hammering ripples across the roof. My ears echo a rattling sound. I search the inside of my ear with my small finger. I hear lizards running across the roof. I call for Grandmother.

A toilet is attached to the kitchen. They added it later, Grandmother says. She does not say who 'they' are, but often she will say, they think we are animals. They make your grandfather work on Saturday. They make us suffer. They built the township. It is crowded in the township. I do not like it here. We live like bees. Who will bury us here? We will die like fruit falling from a tree. We shall bury ourselves. Shadows will bury us. We arrived as people, became strangers, share nothing but our suffering.

How can I cook on my palm, Grandmother says, exposing her hand. The palm has space for a fire, and a place to keep the dishes. The place for the dishes is a flat sink made of zinc, sloping into a hole in the wall where the used water gushes towards the toilet, then empties into the drainage. You have to be careful when you go to the toilet, there are always onion peels and vegetable stems on the floor. Sometimes it smells of rotting vegetables. I hate cabbages. A stoep at the kitchen door, four tiny steps made of cement, kept polished. I sit there counting, sometimes.

The stove is large, made of heavy iron. We use wood for the fire. We buy the wood from the township store. Across its forehead the store says, Goremucheche Trading. Grandmother says the wood should be free, after all, it grows by itself in the forest with no one to help it but the departed. But they sell everything to us here, she says, they sell water. They have taken the water and hidden it somewhere. We open the small kitchen window to let the smoke out. We open the door too. The kitchen door is loose on its hinges. It creaks despairingly. We leave it open all day. Grandfather pulls the door when he comes from work. That door makes my ears sing, says Grandmother.

The tiny kitchen is black with smoke. Soot gathers in the corners of the room, hangs below the roof, creeps out of the crevices on the walls, falls into the food while we eat. The stove sits patiently beside the small window, squeezed at the far end of the kitchen. There is an oven too, with a small but heavy iron door: D o v e r. Grandmother uses a large metal hook to lift the door and place the food inside the oven. The stove is very hot.

From the stoep I watch Grandmother cooking. She calls for me to bring some wood from outside. I like bringing the wood. In the mornings I clear ash from the stove and carry it outside in an old metal dish. I throw the ash into the garden. It puffs angry whirls that climb into my hair. I throw ash into the hedge. It settles a grey cloud over the hedge, very quiet. I find a little piece of wood, only half burnt, and I return it to the stove. Sometimes I find a red glimmer under the grey ash. Once exposed it burns quickly, and dies.

At night Grandmother leaves the door to her room slightly open, leading to the room in which I sleep. It is a small room. Most of the family furniture is stored here; a large table made of wood. The table fills half the room. There are no chairs around it. I can smell one of its legs while I sleep on the floor near it. It bears no cover or polish. That table has brought the forest into the house, she tells me. It smells like a tree. In the morning I fold my blankets neatly, walk carefully around the table, and place them in Grandmother's room. I am shorter than the table. When I have woken under the table, I think the house has shrunk even further. I crawl out and fold the blankets into a small heap. I sit on the blankets waiting for my grandmother. I watch my grandfather leave for work.

On the table sits a rusty sewing machine. Grandmother oils it, dabs margarine over it, polishes it with a small cloth held tightly between her fingers. She makes it run a few stitches, then the thread sulks and

24

breaks. She mends an old dress. Often she just threads the needle. The thread moves through many different hooks before reaching the needle. Grandmother is very careful tracing the path. She bites off the end of the thread, smoothes it with her tongue, rolls it gently between her fingers, then holds it quietly through the needle. She tries twice, tries three times. A ball of white thread sits at the top of the machine, turns frenziedly when the machine is moving. Across the bottom of the large black handle, in gold: S i n g e r. Sometimes I remove the cover very cautiously, my heart beating rapidly: S i n g e r. I run outside.

Grandmother's room is very dark, with a small window on one side letting in the sun. The curtain is frayed around the edges. Old, almost transparent, it captures shadows moving across the hedge, on the road. The window faces the road. Snap . . . snap . . . a sharp trimming round the edges. The scissors have an orange handle. That looks better, Grandmother says, to the curtain. The curtain leaves the bottom part of the window bare. Every morning, before the curtain is fully drawn, an oblong white light waits at the centre of the room. I see it when I bring my blankets. I walk over it and the light folds into my eyes.

I stand still and the light grows warm over my arms.

≈≈≈≈≈≈

# 6

*V*aGomba never opened his eyes again, but fought the blindness with what he had already seen from the earth. He knew the earth and all the varying lengths of its shadows. Muroyiwa grew in this blindness which sought light. He was the last child of his father. He heard the details of this death from his mother who whispered to him around the cooking fire when there was no one else who would hear. Whispered about the fateful root and its ire of lightning, the forehead torn, its edges soft like cotton, the eyes swollen, the eyebrows pulled from their own roots by the drying blood.

VaGomba asked for his son Muroyiwa and touched him across the forehead. VaGomba would say, afterwards, "You have grown." Muroyiwa would retreat from those searching fingers, from the entreating dark hum of the hut, and close his own eyes in imitation of his father's silence. He would try to recognize objects, without light, move towards them and touch them with recognition. He learnt through this that recognition was something separate from sight, from understanding.

Recognition. An aspect of silence, perhaps more crucially of touch.

It existed on the boundary between oneself and the world, between objects, animate and inanimate, rose thin like a coating of milk, equally tasteful, something you could feel on the tongue like an incomplete suggestion, the taste of smoke for example which allowed you to feel flame. Recognition made you feel you had skin separating you from air. It was something like that, to do with skin and bodies, and the abundance of free light. The absence of light could be central to recognition, the hollows of light, laden with silence. Muroyiwa lived in this chasm calmly willing his own blindness, his fingers discovering the hidden edges of things; the soft recesses of sleep, the sharp edges of hunger, and the rounded curves of water held in a calabash which reminded him of death.

His fingers sought the surface of water, not the water itself but its surface. There was such a thing and when he held his fingers above the water long enough, the freshness crept coldly and slowly towards him, rose between the thin air that separated his fingers from the water, then he lowered his fingers by a single exhalation and touched something which clung to him, above the water dry but soft like gathered dust, slightly sticky like honey. This sweetness was the surface of water not the water itself. Not water. There was a difference. He would keep his body resting there, as it was his body he was concerned with, really, more than his fingers. He would keep his body suspended on the surface of water, in that absent light, and this feeling was the tenderest. He waited in a wave of dusty water, soft, gathered from the tips of memory. He felt he had skin. He had woken from a burial pot.

Once he touched his mother's forehead and said, "You have grown." His mother laughed at him. When he was alone, behind the huts or away in the fields he closed his eyes and listened to sounds that would reach him. He heard piercingly when his eyes were closed like those of VaGomba. He heard the air move over his young arms. There was something deep in the blindness of his father, something he could not reach even when he closed his own eyes all day till he fell gradually into sleep. Muroyiwa could open his own eyes at will, if something frightened him enough, a strange sound perhaps. This ability for choice his father had lost forever. "You have grown." His father mistook him for a root in the ground.

There was an intimacy of hostility between the root and VaGomba. Muroyiwa envied this intimate aggression, its attractive violence and the mystery of something banished but permanent, the sound of death in a calabash. Death defeated sight, tamed it to a smooth forgettable memory. VaGomba had courage: Muroyiwa had sight.

Muroyiwa longed to find the root which harboured the sight of his father. One day this root would climb outward to the sun, grow and bloom. The flowers would restore sight to his father.

≈≈≈≈≈≈≈

# 7

$\mathcal{M}$other is turning into a single horrid sound, her voice beaten and lost, her shouts cowering in the midst of her dying. Her voice is crushed, turns into dust, rises in a piercing empty wail. The voice trembles with the end of life. A thin crying through dry crumbling leaves escapes toward me, calls desperately. The voice is wounded, limps sideways, hides. I remember the voice falling down twice, before a final silence. A door closes, very loud. The voice gropes in futile weakened sighs, and fades.

Mother has risen, after falling like that, grief-stricken. I remember her voice shattered, hidden, swallowed by the ground. She walks in wounded footsteps toward Grandmother. Her head is frighteningly bare. She has thick black hair held together by white thread in tight knots that pull the hair from her forehead, drawing at her eyebrows. The white thread twists through her head. Her voice is knotted, unable to breathe.

She wears a cloth which travels around her waist, over her left shoulder, under her right arm. It is tied tightly between her breasts which are pushed cruelly apart, pushed to her armpits.

Mother waits, a wounded stillness, without words to help her waiting. Come inside the house, Grandmother says very slowly, very carefully. Mother enters and sits humbly on the bare floor below the wooden table.

Grandmother's face says many things to my mother, her hands moving here and everywhere saying many unspoken things which the mouth cannot carry, the things of inside, not spoken. She says the things women say when they have met each other in water, seen their faces in puddles of mud. Grandmother looks closely at mother and her looking is her speaking of the things they understand between each other, which they speak and speak, in their silence. Not a word from Grandmother.

Then Grandmother gives mother a large white cup full of water. The cup is white with a black rim. Her hand, giving, speaks and speaks, with the curve of its elbow, with its length and its grasp. Water is good, says Grandmother. Mother drinks. Her teeth are heard beating against the cup, her bottom lip trembles. It bears a red gash in the middle. It is swollen with the suffering which visited her. The cup has one large red rose next to the handle. Mother's knuckles, bruised, rest on the rose. She speaks and speaks with her drinking and Grandmother listens, moving her shaking shoulders forward to hear the unspoken things of her mouth. Mother drinks without pausing, and hands the cup back. Her movements are slow like sleep. She extends her right hand, and places the fingers of her left hand beneath her right elbow. She bows her head briefly as Grandmother reaches the cup, retrieves it from shaking fingers. Grandmother leans forward, her face broken, carrying the heavy things of life. A lonely exhalation, a deep silence. Mother has brought a lingering sorrow, a visit from yesterday.

Mother has spoken, but her face says her mouth is full of the anger which entered her, surprising her. Her face says she has found herself in a forest, lost and bewildered. Her silence, her shattered eyes, tell Grandmother everything. Grandmother shakes her shoulders in another grieved ululation. I have heard the blood in your voice, Grandmother sings.

Mother speaks in a quiet and sorrowful ululation, saying to Grandmother . . . Did he not teach me silence, this husband, that a woman is not a man? I am silent. Just silence to speak my silence against the husband who is not a man but a lizard with a rotting stomach. Like a hen chasing its own shadow he has left footprints which cover the homestead but lead nowhere. He has stolen the light of the moon and its promises of birth. He has thrown a handful of sand into the eyes of his clan as though they are nothing, turning them into insects, carrying everyone, the born and the unborn, in a wave of shame. He has prepared his own burial ground, when the ancestors have not called him. I will begin the spurning for them lest they mistake my silence for betrayal, so first I will bury him like a dog . . . I will not bury him but throw him away just like a dead lizard. Have you fed on the carcasses of dead owls, I ask him? Have you seen the sun forgetting its direction which it has known for many years, turning, in mid-noon, to go back and set where it began at dawn? Have you seen shadows repeat themselves, grow once more where they already grew in early morning? Are these the unmentionable sights you have seen? He has filled my mouth with decay, turning the tomorrow of my child into death, burying her, in the middle of the night. My child . . . her closed eyelids . . . her face wet with tears. I open my eyes wide into the darkness and search for my daughter but she is gone, she has been carried by a dark cloud and when she returns I ask, in astonishment, is this my daughter . . . Zhizha . . . is that the sound of your voice and your crying . . . Zhizha? But there is silence, the cloud has covered my daughter with ash and filled her mouth with death. Her brow speaks the mysteries of deep silent lakes. She speaks in a trembling voice which struggles to speak all the pain of her heart and of her growing. She speaks, in one mouthful of

31

speaking. I embrace all her speaking, all her sorrow . . .

Mother has stopped speaking and looks at Grandmother. They stand together, looking at the things they have spoken. The things they have spoken are spread somewhere on the floor where they were seated. They look and look for them. They stand emptily, without words, and they do not tire of their standing. Their standing is heavy with the sufferings of the earth. Grandmother stands with her arms held over her chest, with an ululating shoulder. Their waiting is silent with no words to accompany it. The words have been spoken. The words have vanished.

Mother whispers softly, calling me into quiet . . . Zhizha . . . she says . . . Zhizha. The one who quietens me, the one who reminds of sleep, the one who comforts. Zhizha, a lullaby for my sleep and my light . . . Zhizha.

Grandmother cries into the night. She cries that the sorrow which has visited has no origins. It is sorrow which has no disguises. We are naked on this earth, she cries. Grandmother cries about the many words a woman must swallow before she can learn to speak her sorrow and be heard. There are no words only sleep and death. Death will always be waiting to relieve one of sorrow, she says. We have become strangers to sleep and our day has no beginning or end. Grandmother searches the night and finds her place of forgetting. This sorrow is like smoke which banishes the trees and the sky. She retrieves a single word, a word too heavy for her, a word which has turned her head white with suffering. Grandmother finds the word and carries it between her fingers, and gives it to mother.

Tonderayi . . . Grandmother offers this word in circling cries. We met in water, she says. Tonderayi . . . she cries again. Grandmother says these are the things for forgetting not remembering. These are the sorrows of life, the sadness for burying beneath the earth, without words. Tonderayi . . . Grandmother cries into her palm which carries this one word from her mouth into our midst. Sorrow is like this, she says, it has no disguises.

*\*\*\**

We live in the township. Each crouching house is hedged. The people are hedged in. An arm swings in a wide continuous slash slicing the air and the hedge. The blade moves sharply downward along the sides, climbs swiftly to the top, moves sideways again, very quickly, then backwards and up above the hedge falling downward, fingers chopped, detached, severed. Slash. I watch a short piece dive upward, turn and turn, fall blindly to the ground where a froth of milk forms, bubbles, is sucked by the earth. The milk is thick and creeps over the long wide blade, stirs, dripping awkwardly down. The hedge is stunted, parted, hewn. Milk bleeds white from the hedge, bleeds slow over the lush greenness, bleeds from fingers fresh and growing climbing upward to the sun, past dense branches, growing boldly, blindingly in a sullen milkiness. Cut cut cut. Milk drips to the ground, surrenders a violent purity. Bright white. Cut cut. Milk drips over a lizard and it darts forward, carrying the milk which flows quickly to its belly. In the brief distance it pauses, breathing hard, while the milk dries over it. Milk dries over its eyes, now slow and languid. The lizard breathes hard on its stomach, moves slowly toward a small jagged stone, waits with a limp tail. Milk pours in thick drops to the ground, along the hedge.

The milk in the hedge is bad, Grandmother says, pulling me away.

The hedge grows again. Green hedge with fingers of thick milk swollen and tender, in branches dotted with tiny angry leaves. I touch the growing shoots. They are soft with waiting milk. I break a small shoot carefully. I turn and find Grandmother standing, nearly hidden. She is singing in a low murmuring voice. I know she sings about me and my mother who have brought this loneliness to her. I press hard and the piece breaks from the hedge. Slash. I hear a knife move through the silence.

Dot dot dot.

White, with milk.

~~~~~~~

# 8

$\mathcal{M}$uroyiwa watched butterflies in the fields. The light poured onto their wings like milk fallen from the sky and they rose in a unison of lightness, in a combined breathlessness, and met the warm blue air spreading beyond the bushes of thorn which carried delicate yellow blooms. The blooms of the thorn trees were like feathers. Muroyiwa saw the butterflies lift from the field and move toward the array of flowering thorn bushes where birds had built their nests. The cloud of butterflies swirled, rising like white mist, lifting like innocence into the air. They moved not far from the ground, caressed the earth in endless enchanting whispers. A distant mountain had opened and released them and their wings danced blooms of sweet light which fell through the shadows of the tall trees. The butterflies were all white, small like drops of rain. Tiny, they spread in an arc like seeds flung, strewn fervently into the air where they would not grow. The arc held them together. The sharp curve of their path fought a heavy wind which threatened to tear them apart. They danced a mute circle around this wind, then quickly and unexpectedly fell beneath it like dry leaves shaken from a tree, fell so near to the land it seemed they would rest there, but something imperceptible blew them from the ground and in an instant they rose, higher than before, and spread their growing arch sideways into the bushes. In a sudden distrust they paused, listened to the light falling eagerly on their wings, then together they whirled into the clean air. Their wings rising and rising and rising in a blur, in a shared sensation of fancy. Their song complete, they rested among yellow petals and thorns, their wings held above their bodies in erect and rounded surfaces, like fingernails. They waited stiff on their wing tips. The butterflies were solid and soft.

VaGomba continued to plant his own fields. He walked to distant villages. He walked faster than anyone in his village. Muroyiwa watched his father's brisk movements. There was something he had to gather from the dust and frenzy lighting the path. There was not much said between VaGomba and Muroyiwa, not much spoken. No instructions given, no expectations raised. VaGomba had no wisdoms to impart. He continued to plough the fields. Muroyiwa followed his father like a breathless shadow. VaGomba sought to heal time, not sight. It was time that had been wounded when he lost his sight, not sight. For healing he sought a rhythm of light. There was an arch that linked the morning and the sunset and he existed within that arch of light. With the arrival of dawn he rose and went to his fields, raising his voice whenever he discovered he had been the first to rise, before VaMirika, before any of his household. "Muroyiwa!" he would call. "Muroyiwa!" That was all. It was enough. It did not matter whether Muroyiwa heard him or not because the call had nothing to do with Muroyiwa, but it was suggested that if this child had woken from death why must adults remain asleep beyond dawn. "Muroyiwa!"

VaGomba cleared the path with a well worn stick. He moved from one year to another capturing light, trapping it with what he accomplished each day, working furiously before darkness became intense. He felt the darkness descend over his arms like cloth, and his arms grew weak, and he could not work anymore. He felt the disappearance of light like a loss of consciousness, like thirst. He woke at dawn and the cloth of darkness lifted slowly, peeling from his arms. He woke in a fine thirst into the shape of the earth and treasured the sound of its stillness, not its quiet, but its stillness. This calm was its being there, his ability to move through it solidly in active anticipation of growth and of harvest. The presence of a life spreading from the dawn of trees and the clamour of birds at morning, was his. There was a stillness behind the clamour for life and a certainty belonging to him, which he could gather with his mouth and cry "Muroyiwa!" He rose in the morning with the light, in the light.

Muroyiwa heard his name in the wind. He did not answer. He listened to the lightness of the wind which held his father like a net. "Muroyiwa!" The wind held his father in a swirling tightness. That timbre of a voice rising beneath closed eyelids, beneath the secrecy of a blind mask, excluded him but brought forth the miracle of his birth. He was birth, somehow, he was what had brought him forth. This truth of being part of an event thrilled him. It made him afraid. It surprised him that his father, in his blindness, was more possessed by this truth and that he saw more of the surfaces of things. His name meandered in the distances and floated with the birds at morning. His name was also a whip, a mockery – of sleep and prepared burial mats.

The secretion of light, to be the source of it. VaGomba accepted the light with his body, not with his eyes as almost everyone did. Muroyiwa could only receive light, not surrender it as his father did, no, not that. So he curled further into sleep and closed his eyes, blinded by the harsh voice of his father calling him. There was a point between the beginning of that voice and the end of it which he listened to, there was no voice to it, only the hint of something not said, a vibration, a touch merely.

One of these positions belonged to him the other to his father. Sometimes he imagined that he was the point at the beginning, other times at the end. Finally, he would open his eyes and watch the light enter the hut, penetrating the thatch. Light had a soft, gentle, determined way of gathering sleep from his eyes. There was a beginning to things, a point so small it could not be touched with memory, not felt, just spreading into the larger things that could be touched and felt. The end of things is also like that, a sort of vanishing which imitates the beginning, impossible to separate from the beginning except for its indescribable faintness. The beginning grows into something; the end into nothing but what has been. "Muroyiwa!" VaGomba dominated the beginning of things and their unquenchable lightness. He gathered death from a calabash and cast it like seeds to the wind.

≈≈≈≈≈≈≈

# 9

$\mathcal{R}$aised, her elbows speak the sorrows which her mouth has buried, which her arms have gathered and hidden, which her feet have harvested in their nakedness. Her arms sway in the rhythm of her silence.

Grandmother says how can we bury the pain which has visited us. It is deep and hidden. This is a tree whose seed has come from unknown lands. There is no water to banish it. This pain cannot be carried in the mouth. There is no mouth. It follows one like a shadow, this pain. It is hewn from rock and larger than memory. How can we carry it on our shoulders. It is swollen like clouds of rain. It is greater than all our yesterdays. It is lightning from a burnt sky.

A woman forgets her name of birth when she meets such suffering, Grandmother says. A woman becomes only a branch on a tree, becomes only a grain of sand. But do they not say even a grain of sand has a mouth to speak. Do they not say caterpillars speak with their many legs. Do they not say that butterflies speak though their wings are only made of dust. Do they not say that leaves greet each other in the morning. But a woman endures, becomes only a memory of all her yesterdays. A woman looks into her dream and discovers a silence with no wings.

Zhizha, Grandmother cries. She folds her arms and her hands along the back of her head where lightning has gathered and weeps. Her arms are silent with weeping, her memory old and far away, folded into some chasm in her past. The air is creased with the weeping of her arms. Tears caress the back of her fingers, gather beneath her arms which release all the living from her voice without giving her the freedom she seeks. Her forehead is unspoken. Her elbows are bruised from her mourning.

Grandmother searches beneath her tongue and finds a word to carry the sorrow which has triumphed over all her forgetting, which has found us. Her eyes seek the departed who have allowed this visit. Her eyes ask why the departed have abandoned our path. Grandmother stands in the midst of such sorrow, and weeps. She cries that she is surrounded by strange tongues. Something has entered inside her dream and buried her. I listen to the silence and death of her dream.

My back cannot stand again, Grandmother says. Our speaking has been stolen. Can morning arrive again into our midst, she asks, her voice longing and desperate.

I know that an unspoken word has arrived and uncovered this silence. I know the word begins with me. I hold the word between my fingers. I hold tight and the word grows deep under my tongue. The word cannot be forgotten. It has grown large roots among us. Branches sprout beneath the ground where memory is watered with death. This ground is stone but something grows on it.

Grandmother says that a woman cannot point to the source of her pain, saying, it is here and there. A woman finds her sorrow in her dream and everywhere. She is wounded even in her awakening. Sorrow is not like clay which is put beneath the sun to dry. It has no shape. It is only tears. Slowly she cries, slowly she weeps, sleeps and wakes. Grandmother touches me with her word. I stand close to her and between us is the far away place we have found, the place of abandon. Grandmother says even though we weep we wait to be remembered and to remember. She says if we wait till morning the dew will visit our feet. The earth has not forgotten us.

Grandmother's song enters into my growing and finds parts of me hidden and still and alone, full of the forgotten things of the earth. She moves nearer to me and touches me with her shadow. The shadow falls from her mouth, falls from deep inside her dream. I am swallowed by the shadow which grows from Grandmother and bends deep into the earth, lifting me from the ground, raising me high. It is warm inside the shadow. It is warm like sleep. I meet the sky in that warm place and the sky is inside Grandmother and it is filled with voiceless stars. The stars fall like rain from Grandmother's waiting arms which fold slowly over my shoulders like something heavy, sorrowful.

I wait for Grandmother to find me, to find all my dreaming with her lament, with her tears. Her song tells me about birth. Her song rises from ancient rivers where the sun no longer rises or sets. A woman will find herself in such a place where memory lingers like the sun, she says. In such a place women stand without trees to surround their weeping. A woman's cry is naked like birth, there is nothing to hide it. It is a place with roots but without trees. Grandmother's song finds the world where women gather. It is a place watered with tears. It is a place of remembrance. When the tears have become a river, morning will arrive even in such a place.

The river will become a tongue. Under the tongue are hidden voices. Under the tongue is a healing silence. I see the river. I see Grandmother. My hands touch the river which grows from inside my mouth, inside Grandmother, grows a murmur and a promise. It is true that a river grows in my mouth. It is true that a dream is also life. A dream cannot be forgotten, it grows roots where silence lingers. It is true there is a word beyond memory, fearless, gentle, full of buried worlds – a word licked with an ancient tenderness. It is true there is a word sweetened by death, lit by a fire gathered from a falling star.

A memory is a mouth with which to begin. We have no mouth, Grandmother says. Only the departed can speak our sorrow and survive. Only they can walk on a path covered with such thorns, such unwelcoming soil. Only the departed can celebrate the end of life and nurture death in a calabash till it blooms. Only they have a wisdom that can embrace suffering. Only they can gather, in laughter and dance, the brightness of the moon and turn it, once more, into death.

***

Mother.

I remember her unspoken sorrow lost and forgotten.

She killed her husband, grandfather says.

Runyararo . . . Grandmother calls my mother's name in the rain. Thunder breaks grandfather's voice apart, and I hear words drop slowly where he stands . . . dead . . . he says . . . police . . . he says . . . Runyararo. The darkness gathers. The rain has entered everything and made it wet. My hands are cold with the pouring water, with my growing fear, tremble with the cold . . . She killed her husband, grandfather says again.

A closing door, thundering loud. Grandfather walks briskly to the small kitchen holding his newspaper like a shield. He is going to read the paper perhaps. It says M a s s a c r e in bold black print on the front, and shows a man with wide shoulders holding a gun. The man killed someone. His eyes are open wide. He leans forward, out of the page. He wears many leaves on his head in a frantic desire to become a tree. The leaves cover his forehead, grow on the side of his face and across his chest. The word of his mouth is twisted and angry, escapes through one side of his face. Grandfather enters my thought speaking to Grandmother with a violent flourish of his arms. He throws the paper into the fire. The man burns. The gun burns. M sac e – the letters curl, curve, break, and collapse. The man loses his angry word. At the end of the thunder I hear a single word, a gasp . . . the word hangs in the room, unable to sit or stand, quivering.

A deep silence, only the rain falling hard on the roof like hooves. Rain streaks the window in a furious descent. Falls like glass. I can hear sheets of water digging somewhere in the yard. The mud flows round and round the house, hitting against the walls. A thick gloom grows outside, spreading. I wait. Grandfather stands behind me. He breathes in the rain, strains to be heard. I look away.

The lightning enters into something that Grandmother is saying about my mother. I have endured, she says. What have I not suffered . . . what have my eyes not seen . . . shall my eyes see more things of the world? Grandmother came from very far, where there were rivers and rocks. She does not complete her thought about the place she came from, about her roots. She wavers and the name loses direction, darts to a corner of the room, hides. Grandmother leaves the place of her birth. She finds her present sorrow large and waiting. Something has dug her past, torn her roots from the ground. She cannot remember the place of her birth. Grandmother's hair is white with salt.

Grandmother places her arms firmly over her stomach and cries about the sorrow which has entered our lives. Grandfather moves away from her wish and her asking but she moves toward him her hands frantic with her calling. She cries about anthills, tall anthills that fill the sky in a land full of dry rolling leaves and rigid grasses. She calls to the unborn, the forgotten, seeks the departed. She calls for her ancestors and her clan. She cries about the yesterday fate of her clan. Tomorrow is not to be known, she cries, tomorrow lives only in the mouth. She cries that she is lost, where is my clan and my people, she asks. The rain falls with the darkness, thunders across the roof, drops to the ground. Have you forgotten Tonderayi, she cries, Tonderayi who was here only yesterday? Do you think I do not know what it is to be conquered by a sorrow which has no name?

The black scarf falls from her head to her shoulders and she knots it again in one quick motion back across her forehead. The top of her head remains bare. An arrogant patch of white hair, exposed, turns her into a spirit which says do you want to see the things which are me, which have entered into my growing and my being? I have been burnt and destroyed and turned into ash but I have lived, even in my sleep.

Her hair is white with the things of the world. She tightens her scarf, moving in slow footsteps toward Grandfather, hoping to be heard. Her eyes are bright with longing, bright with tears. Her voice has lost the long-ago places which are life. Her voice is stone. She cries about being a woman.

My words have lost their wisdom, Grandfather says. He searches deep into Grandmother's thought and retrieves a segment of her sorrow which he rejects with a tall voice that says . . . you have stolen my words. You have pulled my tongue from my mouth. I have spoken and my mouth has been tied by a woman's wisdom.

Grandmother pleads to be heard. I have not spoken, she cries. I ask only for a humble silence in which I can be heard. You have said that a woman cannot speak. I have asked, is it well if I speak the heaviness on my shoulders? I have asked if my woman's voice can be heard, small as it is, is it not your voice too, does my voice not belong to you as I do? Can a woman not speak the word that oppresses her heart, grows heavy on her tongue, heavy, pulling her to the ground? I do not speak and my word has grown roots on my tongue filling my mouth. Will my word grow into a tree while I water it everyday with silence?

Grandmother kneels, hands cupped, arms raised, head bowed, eyes closed, shoulders limp . . . but grandfather says something about my mother in prison, and Grandmother turns away.

Everywhere the wall is damp with the water.

≈≈≈≈≈≈

# 10

$\mathcal{T}$he only shelter for an insect is colour, its ability to merge, to meet indistinctly, to exist without any flamboyance of difference. The guarded paths of ants leave serene traces on the ground, like faint whispers. Here, there are no remarkable footsteps, no phenomenal shifting of the ground, simply a peculiar disturbance easily forgotten. The quiet outpour of sorrow is also the strength of human beings, to leave no resounding echoes or footsteps, no memorable silhouettes.

The sweetness of secrecy became apparent during the war. Secrecy did not mean to hide, to be in a small place. It meant being in a naked place where it was possible to be found. One had to be unremarkable, somehow, silent as death. It was necessary to be inseparable, to embrace torture and despair and clouds of burning trees, to laugh a laugh that was also a fulfillment of fear. It was the similarity between voices that was crucial to living, to creating a landscape spoilt with fear, made pure with subdued desires. There was a chastity which surrounded its birth and a rigidity necessary to its completion, to its consecration. Not spoken, not loud enough to be heard, therefore not understood. Suspected, whispered from palm to palm, passed on to the young in sonorous chants. But chants are not words, they are part of the camouflage which buries words. Chants induce sleep and make mistaken identities difficult to discover.

There was happiness to hide the tears and more tears to hide the happiness: a lie to protect a truth, to tend an untruth. Insects survive during a war, creeping in careful caress, and for a temporary release and procreation, flirting dangerously in a spill of dust. In the tranquillity of war those who burrow the earth in mimicry and pain, like insects, in a protection for life, possess the foretaste of freedom. From palm to palm.

Tachiveyi vanished. Muroyiwa thought of his brother disappearing like a point of light dying in the distance, swallowed by water perhaps, like the outline of a bird at the top of a mountain, like a stroke of good fortune, a stone fallen in water. In the ripple was a din of whispers and the repeated rediscovery of his name. He had died and if he returned home then he would have found another birth; in the ripple was the sound of the death of his people and an uncomfortable betrayal of their own surrender; in the softness of that ripple were their desires spinning in wider and wider waves, thinning into the edges of their sorrow, calling their names of battle. After he left, no one recalled the last words Tachiveyi had uttered, where he had last stood, the last meal he had eaten in parting. Details of his departure receded into the dark cloud that swept their memory to the sky. It had been suspected for days, for weeks, that Tachiveyi would be leaving. The restlessness could not be hidden, nor the triumph of decision. The excitement was like an explosion carried in his arms, for days, and he walked around wounded, healed.

Tachiveyi stopped working in the fields or helping with the harvest. His agony thick like flame, for months he followed the shadows, sitting at the back of the cooking hut, at the front of the hut, under the granary, behind the musasa tree, along the river bank where the women brought their chatter and unwashed bodies. Tachiveyi sat amid their arduous whispers.

He carved a stool which he gave to Muroyiwa. He had never made a stool before. He cursed and carved and worked in the dim light, mostly around the cooking fire. The flame burnt sharply across his fingers and the edges of his knife, but his face was hidden. He tossed fragments into the fire, and bits of words he had chopped from his wood. He whistled a tune between clenched teeth. He made the stool in slow strokes of grey light. The stool was decorated with flowers. It held a lizard. Tachiveyi had removed the tail from the lizard and thrown it into the fire.

He would be gone for several days. He would appear, eyes dancing with the secrecy of escape. He had the eyes of one who is about to die or reveal a secret. Light spread an uneasy gloom in his eyes. Then without solace he left for the war and walked into its blinding black cloud, bleak and harsh. It was a bitter loneliness, with no illusions of a return but the comfort of his own mild sacrifice on the alter of war. An early death, this merging with the future, with the harmonies of war. Those who stayed home were also afraid, but they were outside the shell that contained those who fought, though this shell was thin like saliva.

≈≈≈≈≈≈

# 11

$\mathcal{T}$he house has swallowed death. It has swallowed the suffering of the world.

Green decay spreads through the walls. Curls of paint fall to the floor. Grandmother sweeps the floor with a tight grass broom. Rain creeps through the crevices. In the kitchen, the green has long disappeared, buried in the smoke. Grandmother cleans the house but the decay clings to it and spreads a gloom that descends into the air.

A bus comes to the township.

The bus rests on four enormous wheels. The bus says R O C in large white letters, bright white. The bus is larger than the houses. The bus is deep green, like the hedge, with one long white stripe splitting it. I call and wave as the bus passes by. Inside the driver sits in a deep green overall and I shout greetings to the bus and to the driver. I shout round and round, sing joyfully, turn and turn, fall to the ground, laugh at the wheels rolling and rolling so enormous. The bus driver waves and drives. He waves and drives.

Zhizha, Grandmother shouts and I run back to the house. I hear the bus pass. I hear the other children run after the bus and laugh and shout, their voices disappear under the wheels of the bus. The bus runs over their voices. Zhizha, Grandmother calls, and I run toward Grandmother, toward her voice. I run.

I find Grandmother.

From the verandah, the air is blue, bright with bird-song. People pass by. Sell tomatoes. They collect shoes, repair them, bring them back. Sell onions. They collect empty bottles of cooking oil, in a small cart. The labels flutter in the hedges, bewildered. A bottle rolls from the cart and breaks loud against stone. It splinters, lies still bright and jagged, in brittle disarray. Sell wood. A woman comes by carrying a wide basket on her head. It is afternoon, she says, it is afternoon she repeats more slowly as her shadow reaches us, bends, lowers the basket, kneels humbly beside Grandmother, delivering the basket to the ground. She removes a thin cloth covering the basket. She sells dried fish. Their eyes are glassy and blind. The tails are white, dry with salt. It is afternoon, she says brightly, and her shadow uncurls from her feet where it nestles, expands, swells with the basket, departs. Then a red round hat emerges slowly above the hedge, grows taller and taller till a man in a red and white suit, shouts, extends one arm into the air, rings a heavy bell. He hands me a red ice-cream. I pass it to Grandmother. She says no no and turns her head away.

Do I have a red tongue Grandmother, I ask.

I touch my tongue.

It feels cold and still.

At night, the dogs bark. They have nothing to eat, but they linger. Their howls join in one pitiful crescendo, collapse. Their voices grow and mingle in the vibrating darkness. Voices chase each other up up over the roofs and trees, reduce the darkness into one resounding echo, turn and flee, spread a deathly chorus into the waiting sky. The song is broken, one echo falls on another, tumbles, dies, rolls away, hides in a distant silence. Then a frantic yelp, another effort to ascend, torn, horrid, like breaking bone. An angry call, like splintering rock. Voices circle, collide, race past the night. Then the voices find one more sustained rhythm, very brief, sink in one prolonged cry, very faint, scratching through the air. The township sleeps.

In the early mornings, anonymous voices proclaim the day, journey toward the city. Footsteps mingle along the tarred road. A man shouts. Someone calls back, running forward. The footsteps grow heavy, a voice tumbles forward, greets another, embraces, moves on. A voice runs in the opposite direction. A woman calls, just once. A thin simpering voice. Her steps light and quick. Someone laughs narrowly, in a brief cry. Steps move in a rapid panic, slow down, recover gradually as another reaches them, joins them. Voices welcome other voices. The steps move together, growing faint. *Hokoyo,* someone calls. *Hokoyo,* the voice calls on panicking feet. The word is lost, wanders searchingly through rushing footsteps. Later, a forlorn patter like dropping rain, reluctant, moving forward in chaste unhurried steps. Mingled with the footsteps, a voice sings a protracted sigh.

A heavy cough, then persistent spitting. Another harrowing cough, grating and abrasive. A voice digs through rock, surrenders day surrenders night. Grudging footsteps turn and fall with a trembling hurried gasp. Footsteps approach, find the wounded voice, move sideways, step over it, move quickly past. The cough follows, pleading, trailing and circling a hollow silence. The footsteps vanish. An entangled halting cough, then the voice falling like rock, on rock. A slow rasping cough and the voice rises, moves slowly forward, to the city.

\*\*\*

Grandmother says my tongue can carry everything, even the sky. When I open my eyes there is no sky, only darkness. I must find the sky on my tongue where Grandmother says it is hidden, where my tongue carries it. I must call out the name of the sky till it returns, banishing the darkness. This is how the sun rises from under the land where it is buried. The departed call the name of the sky and their voices send the sky from beneath the earth, toward us. When their voices die, the sky departs from tne earth. It is night. A stone waits in my mouth.

Grandmother says we cannot arrive far into our journeying if we do not surrender our tears to the departed. The journey is long, do not question it. When tears are so many even death can visit. Suffering is not death. Suffering can be carried in the mouth, not death. What has arrived cannot be banished like the footsteps of a hen which can be swallowed by the wind.

Women are children, Grandmother weeps. Our arms do not grow many like the branches of trees. We are children because our arms are so few. Perhaps trees dream of carrying many burdens. Trees have many roots but they do not have tongues to speak their dreams. Perhaps it is better to have many arms to carry your pain and no tongue with which to speak it. We have tongues. We are not trees. Our tongues carry all the memory of our pain. Our journey is watered with tears but we are not trees. Our arms are not silence. We know the way to the river even if grass grows overnight and covers our path. The path to the river is buried on the soles of our feet. This path has many thorns, but it is our path. This path is narrow but it is not death. Even the rain falls on this path which is why the grass grows again on it. The grass does not grow on our feet even if we walk across swollen rivers. Tears have fallen on our feet and watered them, but the grass has not grown on our feet. Our feet keep many journeys. Why must we be silent when we are not trees. We have tongues with which to dream.

A woman cannot let her child rot on the ground. A woman is not a tree.

Women are children because they remember birth. If women are children, then children have tongues.

Grandmother pulls a word from her mouth and places it under my tongue. I feel fingers reach beneath my tongue. Grandmother's word grows and her mouth trembles with the word she has taken from it, that she remembers.

Grandmother touches my forehead with her tongue.

I touch my forehead and find the word Grandmother has given to me. I carry the word between my fingers. I know she has given me a word from long ago, a word that she has retrieved from an anthill. The word is covered with ancient soil, with all her memory. Grandmother buried a word in an anthill before I was born. It is a word that brings all our birth. It is a word filled with water. She buried it after rain had fallen for many mornings and nights. She buried the word to ease her suffering. When she had buried it she returned to the world and gave birth to my mother. Grandmother's arms are heavy. Her arms carry many words. A word is like a wound that has dried, she says. Runyararo, Grandmother says giving me the word of her beginning. Grandmother brought this silence from a burial ground. The silence gave birth to me. Runyararo is my mother. My life began in an anthill where Grandmother buried one word and found another. Runyararo, she says. I know this is her word for burying the heavy things of the earth. I long to know the word which banishes silence, the word which follows her everywhere.

I see an anthill. Grandmother is inside the anthill. Under her tongue is a word. I wait under the tongue. I wait for Grandmother. If I do not remember the word I received from my own mother then Grandmother will remain hidden. I do not remember my mother. I must remember the word. I must remove it from under my tongue where Grandmother has placed it and return it to her. Grandmother has given me the word and I know it is a gift beyond life, beyond the known places of the

53

earth, beyond all sorrow. My tongue is empty with no word to free Grandmother. An echo is not a word. An echo is the end of a word. After an echo is silence. I have swallowed many echoes.

Grandmother says a woman must not swallow her tears. A woman is not a tree. My arms reach toward Grandmother. She has given me a word which only a woman can give to another, give back to another. This is a place where women harvest. I touch this word and feel it on my tongue. It is a word heavier than the stone in my mouth. Grandmother says words are like that, sometimes one retrieves them from places that are forgotten, places that one has vowed never to revisit. Some places are long ago. When sorrow has visited, a woman will return to a place she thought had become memory.

A word does not rot, she says. It is not a fruit that rots on the ground. A word does not rot unless it is buried in the mouth for too long. A word buried in the ground only grows roots.

≈≈≈≈≈≈≈

# 12

*T*hree years after Tachiveyi left, Muroyiwa went into the mountains. He travelled to Njanja with a hope of encountering something separate from war. There was no rain in Njanja and VaGomba had stopped ploughing the fields. He now carved stools. He carved many of these stools which had lizards with no lizard tails. He felt with his hands, and carved. His stools were more perfectly made than the one Tachiveyi had carved.

Muroyiwa had heard that the war was intense in Umtali, that people did not plough their fields because there was so much dying, not because there were no rains. It was difficult to grow anything during a war, to tend something which had life and a tender root offered to the soil. Muroyiwa wanted to find something which was separate from the war. He would find it there where the war was. It would be something benign, so harmless it would be impossible to miss, a feeling, perhaps, something he could touch. There was something unscathed, restorable, untouched. There was something mild as milk, mute, but not dead. A sound merely, a gesture from the sky, a singular sight. There was something.

He imagined his brother tearing off lizard tails, instead of fighting. He imagined flowers blooming amid signs of death and silence. Muroyiwa had never seen the mountains.

He arrived in the mountains and it was like falling into a great depth that seemed to alter histories, change an entire past. So towering were the mountains Muroyiwa forgot everything, particularly the war. It was the war which had a tender root to the ground, which clung to the mountains. Muroyiwa felt light and floating and insignificant. He was not important at all. He was trivial like an insect. He did not have a tender root to the ground, like the war. It did not matter if he continued living. The mountains had a life away from his own, separate and supreme. The mountains held him in a repose of sleep.

On the first day that he was there the mountains reached out and touched the sky with a smooth shelter of comfort, not death, those mountains swayed into the horizon, not death. The mountains greeted him in rolling green hills with feathery clouds descending, freeing those mountains which were high in the sky though the sky looked low and swaying, there was something like comfort held between the sky and the earth. The clouds were white and polished, clean with no memory of death. The clouds were clean like water. They washed over the mountains and released a pure light which lit the hills. Between the sky and the hills was light spreading and soaking into the earth. The hills were thin with the light from the sky.

On the second day the light and the mountains vanished. There was land stretching flatly into wide dark ripples which met no sky, there was no sphere of light holding the edge of life, no horizon to nurture opportunity. There was despair, undulating like naked waves where the mountains had towered with simpler grace. The clouds were black and blew like blinding ash into the eyes. The clouds were powdery and swirled dust over the mountains which retreated and shrunk into angry mounds of arid earth. The mountains emptied into the curling dark clouds which pressed insistently upon them, and the morning was dark and held a fierce magnificent calm. There was something like grief held tightly between the clouds and the mountains. The clouds tore and dropped into the mountains, then spread like a spray over them, like dry rain. No light just a tearing behind the clouds and they released the thick mist, black, which had the appearance of something crushed into a delicate pain. Muroyiwa held this black dust in his eyes, this black light which had unbearable grains of grief in it, then held his eyes together till he found the tender root which linked the war to the mountains.

The darkness swelled. This gloom made no sound as it fell and greeted the ground with dense layers of cloud. The dance of the clouds was a quiet release of fine dust pouring downward into these barren and bleak hills which waited, teased with the promise of morning. In the pale grey of this sky wrapped with gloom, with war, Muroyiwa stood blinded by a surging darkness.

The absence of light.

≋≋≋≋≋≋≋

# 13

*I* dream of the moon. I dream of mother, Runyararo. The space is in my head, somewhere hidden. There is only one word kept safe in that secret place: "Tonderayi." I hear my grandmother say it. Grandmother carries the moon on her face, bright and lingering. Her eyes are closed. She hums a lullaby, about flowers opening, greeting the sun. The lullaby grows faint, wilts, dries up. She sits very still, and I hear her mutter, "Tonderayi." I take this one word from her mouth, pull it out like cobweb, and put it in a safe place. When she needs it I will take it from the safe place and give it to her. I keep it safe for my mother, too, because she says words are precious, like drops of rain, like milk. Words can heal old wounds. I remember mother, I remember her words. I turn toward her, move close to her voice. I show her my old wound, on my knee, a tiny scar.

The sky is dark and near, I can almost touch it, except I am frightened. A dark cloud grows toward me, above my head, moving slow and near. It is carrying a lot of water. But it is dark, like smoke. The water in it is very old, says Grandmother, the cloud has been carrying water from yesterday.

My voice trembles, dries, beneath the cloud.

The cloud is full of waiting. It awaits the moment of birth, then it pours water to the earth. The cloud is dark with promises to the earth. The rain is dark in its promises of birth. Full of giving Grandmother calls from somewhere beneath the lemon tree . . . Zhizha . . . Zhizha. But I see the dark of the cloud descend low and drop over my head in a slow depression blinding my eyes and I shout down the tree and I fall, hard on the ground, down on my knees. It is a long way down and there is blood on my knee, dark red. Grandmother says

Zhizha, do not fear the clouds.

I show mother my old wound. Mother touches my knee and says I am too young to know of wounds. It is a bad thing to carry scars. There are no words for certain kinds of scars, only sorrow and forgetting, she says.

I keep the cobweb word I have taken from Grandmother's mouth. I will give mother the word. Mother will heal her scars, her old wounds. I will give her the moon to carry on her face, like Grandmother. Perhaps Grandmother too will forget the word and I will give it back to her, perhaps I will free my mother from her journeying, perhaps she will remain with me, perhaps I will remember the moment of my birth, remember the way I cried, just like mother and Grandmother.

I see Grandmother bending, looking frantically around her, beneath the bed where I sometimes hide, and I whisper, very softly, "Tonderayi". She turns round, picks me up from the floor, holds my ribs tightly, asks very meekly,

What did you say, Zhizha?

Her voice is slow and searching full of unremembered things. Her voice rises from silent worlds. I have stirred the cries of her silence. I have found the lake of her sorrow. Something has flown from her eyes, dropped from her chin, departed. I keep my silence to protect her trembling voice and her shaking arms. It seems to me that if I say the word again, she will drop me to the ground and die. Her eyes turn yellow with tears, and the skin falls from her face and dries up, all at once, like lemon peels left all day in the hot sun. I see her forehead spread into the edges of her face, as though something pulls at her from behind her ears. I see white hair framing her forehead, twisted, full of salt. Then I see her lower lip shiver, with tears. I hope never to see my grandmother look like that again. I am frightened.

I do not know if Grandmother remembers my face and my voice. I curl my toes beneath my feet and wait, wait to be remembered. The salt has left Grandmother's hair. It traces the top of my lower lip. I taste the salt on my tongue. The salt falls in drops from my eyes. I feel the salt falling. I do not move. My arms are still. I do not swallow the salt or Grandmother's cobweb word. I look at the silent shadow. I hope the shadow will surrender Grandmother soon. The shadow has swallowed Grandmother. Shadows are silent, carry many secrets.

Grandmother's eyes say she has forgotten me, that she has left the things of this earth. I do not cry. I hold the hidden word tight in my mouth and look at Grandmother. I long to know what it is that has brought this dryness to her face, this torment. I long to pick one ray of light and spread it across her forehead, but I do not know how. Then she places me helplessly, shakily, on the floor . . .

What did you say?

But again I resolve not to speak. I feel deeply that I have betrayed her. I turn away, knowing that she remembers me and the word that I have stolen from her. I have seen her hidden world, her place of forgetting. I decide never to give that word to my mother. I decide to take the word and hide it, somewhere where Grandmother will never find it again.

Grandmother stands under the green heavy leaves of the lemon tree.

She stands there till the sky is dark and there is nothing left but the lemons going dot dot dot through the sky. I watch her, sorrowful, amid the lemons so bright. I wonder about my mother and my grandmother. I wonder about the places they have travelled. I wonder about the words they have given, hidden, stolen, for each other. Zhizha.

I touch the wound on my knee: my scar, my hidden world. I bend my knee and my scar widens and curls beneath my knee. I pass my thumb gently over my scar. I hide the word I have woven. Grandmother says I fell before I had learnt to remember. When I was born my eyes did not know how to remember. After I learnt to remember I fell down again, and my scars taught me to forget. Scars are our hidden worlds, our places of forgetting. I fell from a lemon tree. The tree had many thorns.

Grandmother holds me close to her breasts, saying, the things of the earth are heavy my child. Zhizha, she says, very quietly. I listen to her silence and her dreams. I know then that I have the power to save lives. I never say that cobweb word, after that.

I long for silence. I long for the silence of mothers and grandmothers, their promises of a blissful remembrance. I linger, in my joy and forgetfulness. Grandmother tells me of birth, of the things which happened before I was born, before my mother was born. She tells me of her child buried beneath an anthill, tells me, of her cobweb word.

\*\*\*

Silence has endless roots. Grandmother gives me her word for remembering, for burying the torment of the earth.

Tonderayi . . . she says, her eyes held tight as they search. When pain is too much for the shoulders to carry, words become like dry leaves.

I remember your grandfather's words like uprooted trees, she says.

Your womb is rotten.

I married a womb filled with termites.

To remove the waiting from your grandfather's eyes, I waited too. A boy arrived into our decaying like one drop of cold rain and the waiting left the eyes of your grandfather.

Zhizha, birth is a soft cold touch like memory. Like drops of water on the back of the hand, becoming warm. Birth is like a beautiful feather wet with rain then covered with sun spreading once more over the palm, a blissful lightness tugging wondrously at the soul.

The birth of my son, Grandmother says into her memory, into me. I watched that drop of rain descend from the sky trembling and screaming, preferring not to reach us, not to surprise us. He never grew. He will never grow. When he arrived, all parts of him refused to grow except his head. His head grew and grew, a drop of rain that had lost the serene gift of flight, of its shimmering reflecting surface. I was frightened. His head grew with my fear, filled my arms and my heart and my song. They said his head was filled with water.

The water kept growing inside him, moving and turning, filling out into his eyes, in his dreaming places, silencing him. He will be gone in a week, they said, so gently. He will be carried by a river. You cannot save him. I cursed the Sabi the Hunyani the Limpopo the Zambezi the Mfuri . . . then I prayed to the departed for forgiveness. I turned from the wrath of ancestors and prayed for drought and starvation. I sent ululations to the earth, praying frantically.

Into his mouth I placed my breast, swollen with desperation, and he drank. I was afraid. He sucked the pounding of my heart and its rhythm. I would kill my own son. He would die from the pounding of my heart.

If you do that his neck will break. His head is too heavy. Do not embrace him. Do not give him a name he cannot hear his head is filled with water his head is filled with water his head is full . . .

So I knelt over him and fed him, and his head grew a growth so magnificently painful. He sought the rain cloud that had brought him from the heavens and separated him from a harmony where the silence was an echoing of life. In the sky water-filled eyes saw with longing where water and silence were held together.

Sorrow is linked to sorrow.

≈≈≈≈≈≈

# 14

*T*he butterflies were spread between the darkness and the light, each a round yellow which fit immaculately into the hand. The yellow was spotted with black drops and so the wings were stained with flame. Heavy drops rested on these fragile wings and pulled the butterflies to the ground but the yellow shone like something tossed and turning slowly with life. They flew near the ground and could not easily raise their wings. They moved in laboured strokes gathering light while the proud spots spread on the wings which were newly hatched, and frail, and impatient with the desire for flight. The butterflies fell up into the sky and the spots were a multitude of darting insects captured in a net of vanishing light.

Runyararo noticed the butterflies from where she was weaving the mat, beneath the asbestos blue of the house which jutted to the right side facing the narrow street and sheltered her from the screams folding round the house from the back where the children played and cast spells on each other which made them drown. She could hear the rough stretch of their voices, harsh like maize husks. They clapped their hands to silence appetite, they made whistles from the hollows in their teeth and bit their lower lips to gather thought. They chased birds from beneath the roofs where they had built their nests and told them to fly simply because they could fly. Then regretfully they picked the eggs from the abandoned nests and held them well. They absorbed the warmth and secrecy of these perfect and harmless shells. They climbed back to the roofs and placed the eggs back in their nests and stood further away waiting for the birds to return, in vain. The birds, which hated disturbances and strange interludes, would not return. They failed to recognize the eggs as their responsibility, so they hovered softly in the sky, above the roofs, and swept away to somewhere. The unfamiliar scent the children left had wrapped a mystery around the eggs which the birds cared not to discover. They abandoned the nests and flew in cries limp with loss. Again, the children bit their lower lips to gather thought.

For Runyararo, the mat was like a heavy cloth that spread from her waist where she held it, over her thighs and legs, and nearly touched her feet. Her feet were bare. Her legs were curled modestly beneath the heavy cloth, the mat which was brown like the earth somewhere, not here where the earth was black clay and closely held like a secret. There was something missing in this earth, a certain softness that could nurture hope. This soil was dry clay but it did not matter, only lonely cries and hungry murmurs and insatiable hostilities flourished between the corroded walls of the small houses. Red roofs, yellow roofs, blue roofs. It was a release the bright colours the people spread repeatedly over these squatting shelters. The canopy of intermingling shades shone against the blue sky and tempted despair.

It was a wonder where the paint came from, how it was purchased or stolen, but it was shared like sorrow and held the people together. Holding hands without touching, this was it. It was not true to touch, not true to compete with clay below them which held tight and vibrating.

From the roof tops going up there to the sky was a firm hope even if the rain had also disappeared and only the sun sent a brilliance over these roofs, there was hope because it was empty in the sky and they could each raise their arms up to trace an outline of opportunity above the roofs, above their heads, above their bodies because their bodies were part of a despair that did not rain, but flowed. Their feet were swollen through hours of factory work, their fingers blistered, their waistlines frail to forgetting. There was nothing down here on this firm clay except a trickling of desire caught between the tattered skirts of women who held large torn baskets over their heads and sold what they could, lived what they could. Dried fish, mostly, from somewhere where a river broke the earth or some water hugged the land. Somewhere.

The clean sky above, high and bottomless. They planted hope anywhere but in the ground where it should grow, they planted it in the sky. Down on the ground where they stood, there was just the dry clay, the children throwing stones, running naked and splashing in the ditch water where the dead man had been found. The children had violent creases on their foreheads and swore at sunsets and anything which promised an ending; sleep, unwashed dishes, police sirens, rotting fruit, ripped car tyres, disused houses, abandoned shoes, broken needles, fires and farewells.

There were discarded bus tickets fluttering in the wind and stuck against the walls together with a few torn promises not yet buried, then the empty laughters feeding hunger, nourishing the desire to fly above the rooftops to that place free, clean, not anxious and tight like the clay which kept them captive. So they watched above their heads and waited while flies visited the ditches and licked the dead man's face, while the children laughed and licked the sleep off their throats then tossed cigarette ends which they had picked between the houses, tossed them over the dead face which did not remind them at all of their fathers.

They had no fathers most of them, nothing you could call a father.

The township was a crumbling place with no edifice to it, no foundation but necessity itself. It had always been crumbling like any other place built without rhythm or consent. The houses were slanting, with no backbone to them. They fell toward the setting sun as though the ground had tilted forward to spill some long kept hate out of them. The houses had been built for those workers at the nearby mine and at the many stores in the city centre. Some worked at the factories that formed a shelter of dark smoke in the distance and others at the railway tracks which brought a trail of viscous smoke through the town and carried various goods. Some did not work at all but they stayed in this place and waited for something completely ordinary to appear. The township housed workers, not families. The people had been wooed from their villages into the township but others had been born here in the din of misery.

The walls of the houses had been painted white a long time back. Runyararo did not remember when the houses had been painted white and now after the years the whiteness had found kinship with the clay, welcomed it then freed it in grotesque patterns. The white had completely disappeared. Instead, it looked as though something poisonous had been spread like paste along the walls. A dog could be seen sliding weakly along a wall, and in the evenings, the smell of sewer water tumbling into the ditches. There was a smell strong with certainty.

Runyararo crossed one arm above another, her right fingers over her left arm which was scattered with dots of water that fell from the reeds she was weaving, she pressed the thin reed into a smooth needle and turned it into the waiting length of cloth she had already woven, along its edge where it would grow. Her left arm waited patiently while her right hand caught the thread underneath her left arm, under the mat, and she pulled it to a tightness that spread over the entire length of her left arm, and she felt the stretching along her shoulder and held the thread tighter still so that her fingers pressed hard again along the cloth she had created. Her right arm pulled the thread but first she dipped it once more into the small basin of water which stood to her right and as her hand rose toward her forehead in a tight arch that pulled the cloth toward her chest, the water fell onto her lap and across her left arm as she passed over it to meet the cloth. The water was warm and she did not mind it. It formed a comforting smoothness over her legs underneath the mat, the cloth she had woven.

The mat grew over her legs and she paused and stretched her arms. She released the something which had folded under her arms and upon her shoulders, a certain cloying tension. She felt her legs pull underneath the mat and she raised the mat and shook it away from her. It smelt like something old, something not easily forgotten. It had a deep smell which was different from the ditches that surrounded her, the ditches where a dead man had been found only last night. These small deaths did not surprise her. She had grown in the township and knew that the ditches harboured not just stale water.

Her mother had come from some place where she had learnt to sew mats. Her mother had taught her to sew mats. She said the mats could be made out of anything, even the plastic bags they found scattered in the township. It was the making of the mat which was important, the symmetry of mats, not their material. But sometimes Runyararo and her mother found the true material for making mats, and this was a treasure to them. Then their fingers folded into the substance of memories. They bathed in the scent of an original place, a place away from the tight houses of Dangambvura where neighbours could hear each other snore, fight and dream. Her mother said it was not good to hear another person dream. When Runyararo heard about the dead man she knew that he had died because he had heard another person dream.

She had seen him. She with many other faces whose names she did not know. They all stood around the man till a police van came with a metal box and heaved him away. Runyararo wondered whose dream the man had listened to so well that it had killed him.

≈≈≈≈≈≈≈

# 15

*N*ights turned to water, a darkness wet with rain. I am afraid to listen to Grandmother, to discover her places of silence. I know there is a wide lake in her memory, a lake in which ripples grow to the edges of the sky, a lake in which all our grief is hidden. Her word rests at the bottom of silent lakes but she will find the word and give it to me. Finding the word is difficult and fills Grandmother with all the thorns of her growing. Tonderayi . . . she cries once more in her pain and memory. I hear my name carried in her voice. I know she will keep my memory safe.

Grandmother tells me of her son, of her hidden word, saying . . . Perhaps I had filled him with water at the moment of birth while he still slept. Perhaps my cry for help in that time of birth had confused his journeying and he had chosen not to be born. All that water, warm, moving over my legs, joyfully giving. I should have kept him safe, inside of me. His head was full of water. He would never grow, only his head would grow. Place him in a clay pot and bury him. I did not listen to these voices. I waited.

I lay down in a bed of song seeking those ancestral places from which I would learn to part without regret knowing that death is also life. I had been given the gift of death and my method had been to feel scorned and humiliated in the company of my husband. He never went near the child. The child was my own mistake and I had to clear it up in my woman way, with the help of my own kin. One night I dreamt that your grandfather picked up the child and walked into a large thick forest, saying, I am tired of this waiting. He buried the child in an anthill in the middle of a dark forest. He buried the child without my presence, without telling me about it. The anthill began dissolving as though melting with sun, turning into mud. This red earth flowed rapidly following your grandfather through the forest.

Your grandfather drowned in that mud. His eyes turned an anthill red killed by his own son whom he had abandoned. For once, he asked me for help. He implored me to uncover my secrets which would save him. I offered him the desperation that had swollen my breasts. He preferred death. The child remained with me but the dream left me with a strong distrust of your grandfather.

His relatives whispered that the child's existence was evidence of my talent for untold evils. Who among them, they asked, was capable of such a miraculous distortion of birth, such a profound aberration? When they had finished retracing all the flawless histories of their births they shouted in one resounding voice saying that indeed, my powers would destroy their illustrious clan and I must be returned, immediately, to my own kin, with my offspring. Something stopped them. If I had produced such a miracle of birth, was I not capable of willing something similar onto their wombs? In deference to their own fates, therefore, they retreated, still threatening, though in whispers which they made sure did not reach me. They disguised their threats into repeated greetings, but I knew all their natural and acquired abilities for life-denying exchanges.

He drowned.

There were always those who knew and said it was not like death at all, and I should never call it that, for he had never lived.

He has come on a visit, to see the things of the earth.

He has brought water in his eyes.

He is a semblance of life.

She is a digger of graves.

My son drowned one night while he slept. He drowned a fierce drowning. I buried him in the voiceless inside of my heart. He is the son of my ground.

Tonderayi. One who remembers.

***

I sleep, a sharp sleep like a piercing thorn, missing my mother and our belonging, crying in my sleep. Grandmother's voice comes and sleeps beside me. There is nothing to fear I am here, she says. Her voice is filled with milk.

She ties a scarf over my head saying look, there is my little girl. I touch the scarf on my head. It feels heavy and tight. I take a few steps with my head held high. I am Grandmother. The scarf falls off my head to my shoulders.

I wear her hat which she placed on my head one morning saying you are me, you are the one who is me even more than your mother.

She sings a lullaby rich with flowers, saying, rest your calm on my shoulder and your face wet with tears so bright.

Her arms are warm with scented embraces lulling me to sleep. A small blanket folds neatly round my shoulders, round my neck, below my chin.

Sleep my kind girl do not be afraid, do not cry for your mother.

Your mother is strong like the skin over your knees, touch the strength of your mother here on your elbow. I turn in a muffled voice saying, there is only you Grandmother. Mother is strong like the soles of my feet. I turn again from Grandmother's pleading, my tears spreading warm over my ears. Grandfather says we must not talk of mother.

Grandmother says I smell the earth under your arms and the rain smell. She remembers the forgotten things of the earth so old. Her brow is filled with promises of dawn, filled with the distant places of the moon she has travelled.

I see you Grandmother. Where is my mother, is she dead? Grandmother gasps.

≈≈≈≈≈≈≈

# 16

*S*he walked through Dangambvura selling her mats which she had rolled and tied together. She would sell at least one of them, before the end of the morning. She walked carefully between the houses and darted among the children who were throwing mud at each other. She saw that the mud had not fallen on her mat, and walked on. Runyararo knew Dangambvura very well. She knew all its sounds and smells, its missing shelters, its lingering anxieties; in the early morning the smell of cheap soap saturating the air, thrown out into the yard in the used water, the stinging smell of Lifebuoy and Sunlight which provided a penetrating welcome. The air possessed a clinging despair which breathed into her and made her knees fold, a bitter smell which made her rub the saltiness off her eyes and kept the tongue heavy and numb. Then as she entered the yard she found a small dish, made out of empty tins of cooking oil expertly welded together, a container beaten to a rounded flatness. The dish was now turned over to dry. A tiny piece of green soap lay safely above it, to dry. There was morning with dreams polluted and doubtful. There was the rich smell of cheap lotions, green and thick and unapologetically present, with names like Girlfriend, Black Beauty and Dawn. It was overwhelming, this smell of cheap lotion.

Later in the day, the soap was swallowed by the ground and vanished leaving only a faint acrid touch to the air, and peculiar shapes on the ground where the water had dried. Entering in proud swells was the smell of onions cooking in oil. The smell of onion mixed with paraffin. A slightly open window released the paraffin into the yard, into the winding streets, and it had a taste to it, of frying onions. Paraffin that you could taste, the smoke in it, the folds of sadness in it, the onion in it. It sparked the appetite because it was food and made one remember though not really want food too much because it smelt like soot gathered in the mouth, like something poisonous wafting into the air, breathed and kept, this paraffin and peeled onion.

Dangambvura was reeling with improbable desires. If not the paraffin then the fires outside and a woman bending over a small pot using the bottom edge of her skirt to hold the burning handle of a pot. On such a predictable afternoon the onions mixed with the fire, cooking and tasting of flame and smoke. The smell of burning onions because the fire was too deep with flame and burnt the onions and the oil, but this was food. And cabbages boiling too. Boiling and spoiling the afternoon with a smell which had the familiar morning scent of discarded soap in it. A constricting smell, suffocating. It was not good, this smell of boiling cabbage. It had a dulling feel, strong with something in it that made the head heavy and turning, something which was cooked to over-ripeness. It was unbearable this smell of boiling cabbage in these narrow streets patterned with stale voices where something else, other than faith, had been resurrected. A whisper of fatality or something equally complete. The windows opened wide, the voices thin, the desires louder than memory. Such were the ceremonies which nurtured Dangambvura.

Sometimes there was a new detail added to a house Runyararo had knocked on before on a day when she had been again selling her mats. This transformation was an attempt at restoring something lost and no longer recognizable. She saw stones placed in a straight row to surround a growing peach tree. She saw that a hedge had been cut, trimmed to evenness. A doll discarded, the hair golden and still shining, its eyes turned to the sky, its arms missing. A discarded wheelbarrow, the metal rusted, with an abandoned litter of cats fallen asleep, not interested in hunger or affection not proffered, not interested in their own abandonment at all, they simply slept while every curious sound visited every emptiness but their own. They slept steadily. Then a burst of peach blooms.

Pink and soft in that dense and dark place, a pink glorious spray of light blossoms floating and endlessly falling. You could pick the colour from the ground like a dream. So tender and trusting, this spread of colour it made you hope and feel indescribable passions, it made the mind clean and hopeful. Such a sensation of simple bloom. When they fell the ground scattered with ephemeral light, tantalizing like quiet rain. Runyararo liked the fragile smallness of these peach blooms. She liked their promise of growth. They were pale and frail and polite. They touched the ground with a soft paleness, fleetingly. When the sun fell more solidly into the blooms they became thin, almost white with their glow, but when a cloud passed over the sun they became heavy and bloomed afresh. Something would grow on them, the strong blooms which remained on the tree and spread daintily over the branches.

Runyararo could already feel the delicate fur covering the skin of the fruit, not yet ripe. The pale green of the fruit, the narrow oval shape hidden beneath the deep green leaves which she liked to crush and bring to her face, briefly, just to remember the smell of peach leaves. The small fruit growing, even that she liked to open and discover the white seed inside, so large and so penetrable she could crush it and peel its whiteness off like a thin membrane. A bright white of seed that she liked to look at and know that in a few weeks it would have hardened, grooved and changed into a solid brown. Only then would the fruit continue to grow, larger, itself hard, harder, then it would succumb to the sun and reflect some of its glow, sweeter, breaking into a tender yellow and faint redness, a smell so good it enhanced the sun and made it new.

The ripe peach split in half and you could see the brown seed inside the fruit because the fruit had matured and flowed with readiness. The brown hard seed which contained all the life of the tree in it. The ripe fruit, so soft when you pressed upon it and the juice ran freely through your fingers, and when it dried, left a sugary stickiness. It looked to the ground, the fruit, split in two neat halves that held together like a question. It desired to fall to the ground and rot there with its forsaken but cherishable ripeness.

Such a tenuous glory, this blossoming and ripening. Then the multitude of magnificent pink petals would be forgotten. Only the smell of ripening fruit with its mellow tint persisted.

≈≈≈≈≈≈

# 17

*This* is the sea.

I pull the crumpled cloth tightly fitted into the mouth of the bottle. The cloth unravels and lies open. I smell the water. I dip my finger in the bottle and taste the water. It has a strange taste, like salt. I spit it out and wipe my finger against my flowery dress. I taste it again. That water can cure anything, Grandmother says. It is full of the things of life. The sea is large like the sky, she says, there are people who live at the bottom of the sea. They are good healers.

Grandmother does not drink from the bottle. She waits. One day she will grow very sick, she says, and die. On that day she will drink from the bottle. She will carry with her the things of the sea in her stomach, she says. No, I say loudly. I think of fishes and reeds. I shout again, breathing in water, saying I have swallowed the things of the sea. I see reeds swaying. Salt in my crying and in my dreaming. I hear the cracking of rock and the sound comes from the reeds, somehow, comes from the water dense and dark like stone. The sea heaves a large wave over me and I hear water breaking rock, crashing into eyes so still. The water climbs high, spreading wide across the horizon. I see darkness and cloud.

No one can hear me shout. The darkness has closed my eyes, stopped my crying, covered me with furious sleep. I close the bottle tight with the cloth. I wonder about the sea. I see the people who live at the bottom of the sea. I see their shadows meet me, greet me, walk away in silence.

I listen for the voice of my mother, which calls to me saying I remember the moment of your birth, you cried in a voice like mine, like my mother's. I listen and feel water move into my ears and close my mother out but she reaches a searching hand into the darkness and finds me, saying, I have seen you my daughter I will always be near. I am in your voice, in the sound of your crying. I am here in your growing feet. I have seen you my daughter. She places her palm over mine and says I am here beside your dream, in the dream growing white on your fingernails. I see a dream grow a brilliant white wide across my fingers, and mother says do not be afraid my young one Grandmother is here, she is our tomorrow. I close my eyes to the rhythm of her beseeching voice crying in my sleep, then I speak, saying something soft into the night. The night brings my mother into my sleep in showers of slow rain bright and clear and I speak again, comforted.

Zhizha, I hear my mother calling in my sleep, Zhizha.

I cry to my mother frantically saying, I remember my forgotten world. I remember the pain in my growing. I remember my stolen dawn. I cried in the voice of my mother and my grandmother. I remember my hidden world . . .

I run outside to pick the lemons which have fallen to the ground yellow and ripe. I pick them till my hands are full of tender yellow rays.

I turn. I see mother, her face covered in dry grass. Black winged ants travel over her arms and her eyes in neat rows that weave into tiny circles which grow into each other, widen over her stomach, whirl and turn in frantic silent steps. The ants hurry over her face, linger over her with rounded eager heads, red, with white transparent sacs. They journey with a hunger, delicate and blind over my mother, climb triumphant, pour out bravely. Mother is still.

My voice falls from the sky.

***

Mother saying in a measured voice, repeat after me
a e i o u
Diagonally opposite the dressing cabinet is a window and through it, the sky trees and neighbours enter the house. Through the mirror birds fly past, sometimes.
a e i o u
I sit very still, reading aloud, repeating after my mother through the mirror filled with our calm resemblances and our hope, with sonorous song, with the quiet rhythm of our sleep, with the sound of my growing. I have discovered my mother's presence, her embraces and ululations of joy. I have found the moment of my birth, of our beginnings.

I have seen my mother.

She moves forward, hands me something held tight within her hand, the secrets in our belonging. We have begun our initiation into each other's worlds, our profuse illuminations. We belong and belong. Our yesterday partings vanish like unremembered dreams, like echoes of stream water, lapping gently. My mother.
a e i o u
I repeat silently. I repeat into the deep of the mirror far where my mother's eyes meet mine. I breathe a warm cloud over the shiny glass of the mirror and write one letter across it. I watch it disappear into the mirror. I breathe again another warm cloud onto the mirror and write the second letter, and again it moves away silently, slowly, and the mirror

waits. I meet her gesture of endless warmth, her brilliant growing love. I meet the radiance of her eyes, and in her tears, I find my past.

I meet her in one motion of elation, a cry like joy in which she, in one tranquil turning says, I have seen you my daughter, I have seen the beauty of your earth, of your growing naked feet. I have seen the eternal worlds between your fingers and the secrets in your sleep, I have heard your laughter and its promises of dawn, I have seen the morning on your forehead and touched your restless hope, I have walked quietly in your sleep.

Mother calls to me in a voice just like mine, she grows from inside of me, saying rest your forehead here on my palm bright with longing, sweet with cherished touch. I have seen you my daughter. I have seen into your dreaming my loved one.

She gives me the moon saying the moon is in my growing and my sleep. I look far into the mirror and the moon travels silent and whole, breaks into small fragments, scatters to the ground in showers of joyful light.

I watch myself through the mirror, my mouth moving in different directions with the letters, my lips move forward when I say u, and sideways when I say e. I like most to say o, my chin moves down, the sound rises from deep in my throat, my breath a sudden stop so near. I sit beside the mirror. I repeat the letters carefully. I say the letters with my eyes closed. I close my eyes tight till tears fall down my cheeks. I feel them tumble, fall, and wet my lower lip. I open my eyes. I write the letters across the mirror with my finger. I paint them in blue ink, red ink, green ink, turn them into cloud and sky. I write and write over the mirror. I write downward, curling the letters round and round. Then I write quickly. I try writing with my left hand.

I sit up straight like my mother, my hands folded across my chest and a frown on my brow and sternly say repeat after me a e i o u, then

I change into me, and I say a e i o u. I remember all my letters. I tell my mother and she repeats after me and I laugh then I repeat after mother who repeats after me and I after her . . . I have turned into mother, and she laughs, because she has become me. The letters flow from me to mother.

My mother's voice is resonant and searching. She says we live with our voices rich with remembrance.

We live with words.

≈≈≈≈≈≈

# 18

*R*unyararo and Muroyiwa shared a small room in Dangambvura. Their room was divided into two indistinct spaces by a short fraying curtain. The curtain had large blue stars on it that were faded and torn. A hard string ran through a seam at the top of the cloth, and collapsed at the centre where it carried most of the weight of the cloth. On each end, on the wall, a small hook with the wall around it broken, held the cloth weakly. The cloth did not reach the floor on either end of the room. One half of the room supported a small bed which was squeezed along the end of one wall. It had a cream crocheted cover. It had large holes through which you could see the heavy grey blanket beneath it. The blanket was deeply laden with coarse thread. The prettiness of the cream cover mixed uncomfortably with the coarseness, it hugged it tightly. The cover also was worn, especially around the corners where it folded over the bed, where it followed the bumpy angles of the mattress and was tucked carefully beneath it.

The bed was made of iron and stood very low near the ground. Some shoes showed under the bed, red women's shoes, a black pair belonging to a man. A brown suitcase with its plastic handles missing had been squeezed to another end and held more clothes that were neatly folded together. The suitcase had collapsed in the middle. The lid was almost torn. When it was used a long strip of black rubber was tied over it. There was no window on this side of the short red curtain with the fading blue stars. Nothing separated the two spaces but the hint of separation, the attempt alone.

The two pillows were very flat with use. When Runyararo and Muroyiwa did not sit on the bed, they took the pillows and used them as cushions to protect themselves from the cold cement ground. One pillow was held inside a torn black blouse. The pillows were hid under the laced crocheting. At the head of the bed, at the corner, were the mats Runyararo had made. They were rolled together and leaning against the wall. A small brown mat had been spread on the floor near the bed, and it was new. It was very neatly made, with pale cream stripes along the border, and deep brown circles at the centre.

There was a solid darkness throughout the room, except at night when a candle flickered through the closeness and made the place whole and discernible. Then the shadow of the bed leapt onto the wall and made the bed larger, and the flame from the candle seemed to rise from the bed. The bed grew and rested angrily on the asbestos roof. The shadow of the mats leaning against the wall split the room much more than the curtain. The shadow was broad. It cut the room diagonally. The candle shortened, then burnt low, and the shadows grew still larger till they vanished with the dimming light. The smaller light made the shadows round and flat, not sharp and peaked like the blossoming flame. There was light in the night because the candle was put to burn, more light than there was in the day when there was sun outside but no window to let it in, only that on the other side of the curtain was a small opening, which often was covered with a sheet of cardboard to keep out the ceaseless footsteps. The people passed very near the house. The shoes underneath the bed, the worn suitcase, stars falling off the curtain, and no light. The smallest light provided a moment suspenseful and empty. The light died. The day vanished with the light.

On the other side of the curtain were the cooking utensils. Runyararo did not cook inside the house. She cooked behind the house where she made a small fire between three solid stones. She brought all the pots into the house even before they were washed. It was a distance to the communal tap and she saved the clean water she had collected for their baths in the morning and for their cooking. The morning began with the dishes from the previous night being washed. They were made of tin, painted to a pale green and hit against each other in the small bowl in which Runyararo washed them. Runyararo washed the dishes every morning while her husband still slept.

≈≈≈≈≈≈≈

# 19

*I* call for Grandmother but my voice sinks, disappears. Mother comes forward with tears in her eyes, saying, I am your mother Zhizha. She stands still, looks into the dark trying to find her mother.

I see mother. She has come to visit her mother and to be mother. I see Grandmother. I see mother.

I watch her mothering strange as her visit waking me from sleep. I am your mother, she says, while standing at the doorway. I do not remember her face or her voice. I have forgotten my mother.

I have my Grandmother, she is my mother. My mother is away, very far away in the mirror, inside the house.

Mother laughs and asks to see the mirror, asks to meet my mother. Anger creeps into her eyes like dirty stream-water, marring the rhythm of her visit. I turn away.

I know she is my mother. I do not recognize her. I long to ask her about the places she has visited, that have visited her face but she hides her tears, raises her shoulders high, and walks through the door, past me. I follow slowly behind her. She turns away, moves to Grandmother's room, sits on the chair beside the mirror and places her face in her hands. I enter the room, quietly, and wait.

I have been here all the time with you. Mothers are like that, she says, they can never be away from their children. I can see you even when I am not here. I am your mother. Nothing can change that, not time not distance not even Grandmother. You are me, she says desperately. We grow together even when we are apart. We belong together. I gave birth to you, my daughter. I heard your first cry. You called me when you were born. I touched you in your moment of birth. You cried and cried in a voice like Grandmother. You were born at dawn. You cried for me and for Grandmother. We held you close. You are strong Zhizha, you are my daughter so strong.

You have forgotten your mother. It is like that with forgetting. It does not choose this, saying no, a mother is not to be forgotten no matter how long her absence. Forgetting just comes and takes away everything. Some things are only suffering it is not good to remember them. To remember them is death. I think of you in your growing. I think of my daughter. I am your mother, Zhizha. I held you after you were born.

I heard you cry in a voice just like mine, just like Grandmother. I had not expected to meet myself in your voice, meeting my own mother, meeting you my daughter, all in one moment. I said to my mother,

Zhizha will never forget me, she carries me in her voice, how can she ever forget her mother?

That is how it was when you were born.

I move back from her pouring words. I am not complete without possession of her memory and her desires. Her voice searches through me. I find a dim spot where I hide, and watch.

Her visit is a fragmented togetherness, a handful of caress like blinding noon dust. Her voice reaches me, lulls me to sleep. I grow toward her voice longing for her to stay, to give me the secrets of my growing.

\*\*\*

I long for remembrance but a darkness grows on my forehead, buries my moment of birth. Mother's voice rises, troubled, toward me.

Zhizha, she calls. Zhizha, she calls again with longing. I long to shout . . . Mother . . . Mother . . . but something stops my crying, something in my throat. My voice is dry and lost. I sink back into sleep, waiting for my mother.

From one dress into another she seeks her profile in the mirror and smiles gently at me. I watch her beauty and her grace and her glowing long legs and bare arms and long smooth neck. I see my arms around her neck just like she asks me, and my heart beats fast, my heart is running away from this eternity of embrace, round and round. Then she turns, suddenly, dropping her garment to the floor and saying to me look at these breasts from which I fed you.

I look at her breasts. The tips are shrivelled, like dried tomatoes, the elongated kind which droop to the ground and ripen in a sudden fury from the top down. I do not want to remember my mother. I think of red broken tomatoes. I think of milk, white and bright, from my mother's breasts. I think of ripe and red tomatoes.

She reminds me of my feeding as she moves to follow my turning face. It is all right she says, I am your mother. She is so certain about giving birth to me and about my part in it. She cries at my forgetting, at the things I cannot remember. This is your milk, she says. I want to give you the things of your growing, the joys we have shared.

A tear falls onto my forehead and I stop turning, surprised, but she has returned quickly to the mirror mirroring us and puts on a red-red dress which she says she would never wear if there was lightning in the sky for she would die so suddenly there would be no moment for remorse or forgiveness and with that threat she leaves the room, calling to her own mother, and I am forgotten, for now.

Alone. I try hard to remember everything that has been because that is my gift to my mother. I move toward the mirror and pick the discarded garment from the floor raising it to my shoulders holding it against my flat chest seeking my mother in me, wondering, about being a woman. I put the dress over my head and it falls over my body, folds around my feet. I stand, looking at the mirror and my mother comes and stands behind me.

≈ ≈ ≈ ≈ ≈ ≈

# 20

*R*unyararo woke very early to sew her mats. She would sit in the half-light of the morning while her husband slept. She liked to work in the morning with the early light. There was a soft light over the houses. There was silence, except often a dog barked, something was heard falling, but there was a kind of peaceful light that surrounded her in her work. She felt the light on her fingers as she worked while sitting beside her stoep. She would have left some water in a small dish the previous night, and this water would have a strange coolness to it that she liked. There was a soft milkiness to the water because it was early morning and some silent smoke had grown over it. She would dip deep into the basin and her fingers tingled with the smoke, and then she would dip her reed in the water too. If she left a bundle of reed in it there would be a certain scent to the water that she liked. This was morning.

She thought of her mother who had taught her about making mats. Her mother lived not too far from her, only a few streets away. Runyararo was sure that she sometimes could see the smoke from her mother's morning fires because her mother was always one to rise early like herself. She liked to stand on her stoep and gaze into the distance thinking of her mother. Her mother had not been happy about her marriage to Muroyiwa but because she was already expecting a child her mother had relented. It was not clear to Runyararo what her mother disapproved of. Perhaps it was that Muroyiwa said he had come to the mountains to look for butterflies. This was not a good revelation to her mother who said a man could not travel from Njanja to Umtali to look at butterflies. It is the war he has come for, Runyararo explained. That is even worse then.

He had said his brother was in the war and he would no longer return to Njanja. He would remain in the town of Umtali and be near his brother. He said strange things about his brother tearing lizard tails and eating them. When he was really happy he told her about the different calabashes in his home in Njanja. Runyararo liked to hear about the calabashes as there were not many in Dangambvura. He said he would take her to his village to see the calabashes. Then he said he had been born in a calabash. This was strange for her to understand but she believed him because he said it with such seriousness. He focused strongly on his birth. Runyararo was happy about this because she was having a child. She liked to listen to him talk of his village because it was a life separate from her own, and listening to him was like travelling to a distant land. She had never left Dangambvura. She had not seen the mountains Muroyiwa talked about, where the war was, though they were not very far from where she lived. But there was never enough money for an unnecessary bus ride, and there was a lot of fear surrounding the mountains, so much sacred ground, and the war.

Muroyiwa had found work in the mines and Runyararo liked that her husband held a job. They could at least have their own place to stay, not as crowded as the other homes around them, where two or three families lived in suffocating closeness. They had a large room and some privacy. There were few men who could find work. Muroyiwa had found work very quickly. The mine-owners always preferred people who had not been born in the towns as they would accept lower wages and work longer hours and be scolded without ever retorting. The people from the rural lands were considered to be good workers and the mine owner was willing to release a worker he had kept for a while, because he had stopped being grateful. So an enmity was built between the town dwellers and those who had just arrived.

Muroyiwa worked all day in the mines, digging at the rock beneath the earth. It was daunting work and there was always the fear of accidents there, disasters larger than themselves. This they tried not to remember or discuss, till something happened, till a roof collapsed and no one was rescued from the rubble. It was strange that the death was so far away and they could not see it or touch it. Then they filled the evenings with fears which would burn their lips for weeks, but they would return to the mines and work, their eyes black and dry with surrender.

In the evenings Muroyiwa would watch Runyararo creating her mats. She liked to work till the evening light vanished. She would sit outside and he would sit with her. He sat on a small rock which was held to the ground very near the stoep and touched the wall of the house. She liked his face with the gold of the dying sun, and he would watch the perfect symmetry of her mats, the confident movement of her arms, of her wet fingers, of her lips. The symmetry of mats between her fingers gently folding, caressing every thread. She would pass the wet thread between her lips to soften it and recover memory and they would both be quiet with no words spoken. She would twist the thread of reed between her second finger and her thumb, rolling it over and over till it was thin and taut and sharpened, then pass it through the thick braids of the mat she had prepared, and hold the braid close to the place she had linked it to, her thumb pointing toward her chest, and the mat held secure near her breast like something precious so she could examine her thread, what she had created; the symmetry of mats. She would spread the mat on the ground and flatten it, her eyes moving devotedly over the cloth, she would touch every part, searching, removing loose threads, pressing away at the unevenness. She would touch the mat with a particular satisfaction, then look up to the dying sun. Muroyiwa wondered at his own curiosity and pleasure, at the symmetry gathered in her face, in the moment they had shared; her wide smile which welcomed him, her eyebrows almost touching and thin like a clean mark on the ground. A perfect shape.

Then the pounding in his head grew to a hum that would only return the next day when he would arrive at the mine, and there was silence in his hands, away from the breaking rock, from the darkness in the mines. He hated that darkness he entered with his entire body and which stole from him, descending, unable to breathe. When he swung at the surface of the rock his forehead filled with the tremor of the earth and the search-light on his forehead dimmed. The light on his forehead searched the surface and found it bare. He was an insect with a single antenna held to the ground. He burrowed the earth with the light he carried.

Returning to the surface of the earth made him free. He always thought of his brother Tachiveyi who was in the mountains. It was his freedom which his brother fought for. He was not ashamed to think of his brother because he had followed him. He felt that he now almost lived with him. It would not be too far to visit the mountains again. But the road to the mountains had been closed. It had been named the road of death because so many people had vanished there. Muroyiwa felt fortunate that he had ever been able to travel there. It never occurred to him that perhaps his brother Tachiveyi had now been killed. If he allowed this thought to carry him, then he would lose his own importance. He existed as an opposite to his brother, the war was an axis which kept a balance between them. Tachiveyi had courage, Muroyiwa had stayed behind. Tachiveyi was the first born; Muroyiwa was the last. Being born last, it was Muroyiwa who had stolen the light from their father VaGomba. Tachiveyi had created the milk which they had both received from their mother, Muroyiwa had dried it. Tachiveyi was at the beginning of things, and Muroyiwa existed somehow at their end. The return of Tachiveyi to Njanja would bring sight to their father. Muroyiwa never doubted that his brother would return. Each time the lift from the mine brought him into the light, he removed the torch strapped across his forehead and remembered that his brother too would return. This was something he believed. Muroyiwa waited for Tachiveyi.

≈≈≈≈≈≈

# 21

*I* hear something crushing under my rib like eggshells where Grandmother holds me and it is painful like the loss of my mother. I hear mother calling me, her voice is small like mine. She turns from the mirror to look at me saying, I have seen you my daughter. She laughs. We met in water, she says. She calls to me again. I stand close to her sunlight, close to her. I wonder about opening my eyes, about touching the edge of her face. I see her smile blissful with our tender awakenings, soft. She enters my thought and says she is only your Grandmother not your mother.

I cry with a delicate longing saying I want my grandmother who smells of lemon rind. I run. I climb up the tree filled with thick green leaves and thorns where I hide. When I come down my mother is gone. An empty wave steals into my thought and I grow dizzy with my emptiness, grow hollow with the memory of my mother's mothering grace and her giving. I long for mother. Grandmother says sh sh sh you only have a fever you will soon be well. She wipes the sweat from my forehead and gives me something warm to drink.

A heaviness grows on my forehead pulling me away into a darkness so complete and I cry, my crying seems to come from my ears. The darkness is taking me away. A brilliant light falls into my eyes like breaking glass so I close my eyes again and creep back into the darkness where perhaps my mother will come and find me.

Grandmother lifts me close to her. She sings about the river and its children. She says the river is wide like the sky and the sunset. In it all things begin and end. The river is horizon and cloud.

I scramble down the lemon tree knowing my mother is gone, swallowing my cry. I shout for mother, like blood in my mouth. There is only silence, then a whisper so faint from my mother, so distant. From far away Grandmother comes again dressed in water, saying this river is life. If you listen closely to the river you will hear a lullaby in its meandering banks, you will see birth. She whispers to me again with a firm voice saying do not count the stars in the sky, their beauty is not to be possessed in one's hand.

\*\*\*

I look for my mother at the bottom of silent lakes. I watch a shadow creep slowly onto her face. I have wounded her with my forgetting, wounded myself. I long for the moment of birth.

Can you spell duck?

d u c k

The last letter sounds like someone scraping at the roof of my mouth . . . kkkkk

I spell the word again, and wait for another word from her. Again, d u c k, but she does not give me another word to spell. To regain her attention I raise my voice very loud, d u c k. She laughs and says, that is good, Zhizha.

Come and comb my hair, Zhizha, she says. With her left hand she extends an iron comb in my direction and a towel to put over her shoulders.

Are you sleeping, Zhizha, she calls in my direction, to wake me from dream. I sleep.

Zhizha.

I sleep.

There is a time of the year when everyone seems to remember me and whispers . . . Zhizha . . . Zhizha . . . very softly, banishing all those absences of my mother with this calling, then I seem to belong to everyone's mouth for a whole season. I am harvest. I am rain. I am river and rock. I am sky and earth. I am Zhizha.

At this time, the air is a sweetness of newly ripened things and I grow so joyous that my spirit soars and spirals, settling into one ray of golden light. My toes tingle in that warm earth as I help Grandmother spread water-filled seeds that are soft and slippery to dry under the sun. These are the seeds that are life, that hold secrets larger than themselves. At the moment of their birth their mothers trusted them with a secret, and they are tender with promise.

Zhizha, the people whisper, and I turn to hear. They are talking about the harvest.

Zhizha, my mother says, come and comb my hair.

I long to tell her that this endearment is no gift, that I desire no portions and fragments of her living. I long for her never to depart. I wish my mother would stay, but I meet her in dream. My heart beats angrily, and I think, besides, she named me after a stranger. A woman turned and gave my mother a greeting. She took her name.

Zhizha, she repeats, and I receive the comb.

I part her hair in the middle from her forehead to the back of her neck, creating a path. I send the comb through her hair. I move slowly in my parting, resting the comb down in her thicket of hair. I move to her left side and comb her hair straight down, comb it seven times. I am practising my counting. After seven I start again and stop at six. Seven plus six equals thirteen. I keep the thirteen and start again. I comb five times. I add that to the thirteen. I have combed her hair . . .

Zhizha. I start suddenly.

Eighteen, I say.

What is that?

Thirteen plus . . .

Zhizha, comb the other side of my head, she says.

She takes the comb from my fingers and digs it abruptly into the hair on her right side.

Tiny black hairs fall against the towel as I comb, parts of her falling off. There are parts of her trapped in the comb. I pull these soft dying parts out and place them in the pocket of my dress, to secure a memory. I have trouble remembering my mother so I work extra hard at it, alert to pick the parts of her which fall in my direction. Between my fingers I feel her hair, this hair which is part of me and of Grandmother. I touch the roots of her hair and at the bottom the hair is a shiny dark.

Grandmother's hair has turned white. Sometimes she says, comb my hair, but often I am the one who says Grandmother may I comb your hair? I begin by parting the hair into two halves just like this and the roots are grey like smoke. Grandmother says her hair used to be black but the world has entered her too much and her hair has turned white.

I remember Grandmother and the feeling is like sunlight on my arms. The smoky greyness covering her head tells me too many things and I refuse to listen, instead, I call out loud to her saying, your hair is dark Grandmother. It is not grey at all. I pull out one black hair from her head and place it in the middle of her palm, saying look. She looks at the hair and says, you are right, this hair is black like yesterday. Then she goes to the mirror and spoils all my dreaming. I follow her to the mirror and stand close to her.

Zhizha, my mother calls, stop pulling at my hair.

With that she removes the towel from her shoulders and looks at the many pieces of broken hair, very closely, then slowly proclaims . . .

You have broken my hair, Zhizha.

Mother, she calls. Mother.

But Grandmother is not home. Mother waits in her thin red dress, her arms resting on the window sill, her hair parted, her eyes clear with tears. I wonder when next she will visit those long ago places which sometimes pervade her face. When she turns, leaning her back against the lower part of the wall, and her head against the window, she says, alluringly . . . Zhizha.

≈≈≈≈≈≈

# 22

*T*hen there was the ceasefire and the women poured milk to the ground and welcomed the men home even when they had not seen them walk back, they sought them, their names and sheltering presences, their pounding hearts and their many scars. The women had a new gaiety in their speech and their motions because something they thought had vanished had returned, somehow, with a scent they recognized as all their own. Not whole, this return. The surrender of weapons allowed the women to linger in their dreams, towards wakefulness, and touch their own lips in wonder. Waists thinned with anticipation, arms widened with joyful longing. They feared absence.

The wounded too arrived, lonely men lost and naked and thick with despair, unable to touch the edges of dream. These haunted many who had been wounded and could not nurture hope. Something about this day had taught them not despair, but shame. They hid their bodies beneath their bowed heads and folded shoulders. But the women sought them from their hiding because these men too they loved and let them in. They waited with their windows held open and their eyes embracing the sky, searching for those who were returning to plant new dreams on the ground, offering respite. The ceasefire meant that fear would be turned into celebration. They touched something in this new boundary, a new taste to joy, a new sound to dream. They rejoiced at the joys that tantalized them. Something. A newness, something hatched, pure and bright with surprise. Something not yet known, to be, almost felt. A touch. The ceasefire had brought them a burst of hope. A whisper, a form, something held in the hand. Perhaps a necessity to living, a longing almost fulfilled, nearly complete. Places that would be their own, truly. A feeling that was shared and felt. A return. Something. Sparks of flame. A glitter of sunshine and incantations in the rain, chants and ululations. The absence of war. A fortunate illumination. Accustomed to fear and loneliness the people wept at the potential of freedom.

And the rain came. And the ceasefire. And the men were caught in the pouring water, but they walked on and threw away their weapons like worthless utensils, in easy courage and abandon. They had no more dreams to protect but their own bodies now scarred and harmless and sweet with passionate ambition. When some of the women offered their voices as shelter they dared not resist. These women had survived waiting. The men tumbled out of the sun, and they had brought women who had fought beside them.

These women had new names that the past did not echo, they had long arms and long legs and long voices. They laughed louder than the men because they had shared secrets with them. The women were strong and looked only at the sky where they said it was free. They would begin in the sky, not the earth. They would begin from there so they removed the yellow roofs and the red roofs and tore them to the ground, with their own arms. They wanted to see something else, not this canopy of painted sky. They wanted to begin without shelter. And as for desire they knew something about that too. This emptiness, these bare roofs. These same women had killed farm dogs, white men and grasshoppers.

Before this bustle of freedom, this ceasefire, ten years before, Muroyiwa had met Runyararo. Their child Zhizha slept in the room which had been created by the curtain with fading blue stars. In this tight space their lives would change completely while the war was fought and anticipations conjured.

Runyararo would be among those returning home from another direction altogether during this ceasefire, released, able to see her daughter again. She would miss the laughters shared by the returning and not see the battleground where a new belonging was talked of and understood, the wonderful rhapsody.

≈≈≈≈≈≈

## 23

$\mathcal{M}$y eyelids fight against the encroaching darkness. I turn and turn in my sleep. Night fills with the sounds of insects growing into the darkness, shrill whispers pitched in cries. I hear a vibrating call, a screeching sharp and persistent, followed by a chaos of whispers which prolong the night. I turn in my sleep, a chorus of sleep.

I wait for daylight but something carries me away into the darkness, into sleep. I drift in a bed of uneasy suspicion, and in my dream I meet myself participating in a ritual of death, dancing across a field of burning stumps. A shadow crosses my face and wakes me, but because whatever has chosen this night for its purpose intends to triumph it exerts its power over my eyelids through my sleep and I return to dream. A trembling sleep. I sleep a restless sleep travelling through mountains and rivers, through dark ominous skies, through hidden burial-grounds, through groves of tangled trees. Then I wake suddenly, because some sound has reminded me of a deep oncoming sorrow but because it has already been a night of sleep and wakefulness I turn again, and sleep. A smothering sleep, like death. My brow is wet with dreams. I turn and turn, longing for daylight.

A muffled cry struggles in the dark of the night followed by a silence so final I sleep. The cry rises again pitched and intense, from within me, circling high over my head, turning into a thick shadow. Again, I succumb to a deceitful sleep. A piercing scream enters my dream, moves past me into the darkness, climbs high in the sky. A shattering trembling scream from deep inside me, of blood and water in my crying. The shadow enters into me, enters my crying, covers my eyes with a heavy hand. My brow is wet with tears, wet with fear. My heart beats hard on my chest, seeks my dream and my waiting, banishes sleep. I hear my cry plead in the distance, then grow into a meander that leads farther into the darkness. My cry is silence and death. Night descends firmly into my wakefulness. The sound follows me, struggles to enter, pulling hard at my limbs. I descend deep into the earth. I struggle in the darkness.

I will die from the pounding of my heart which does not allow me to bend or move my arm but turns me into stone, fills my mouth with dry leaves, covers me in decay. My voice is caught in the midst of its awakening, unable to escape. My voice stands upright, a solid thing somewhere between my breasts splitting me in half. My voice seeks the moment of my birth, the secret in my name, the promise in my belonging.

I cry in my sleep, this sleep of death. Tomorrow has departed never to return, death has entered my dreaming entered my growing turned it into mud, and now I cry in one small whimper, cry quietly into my memory saying, whispering, I am the opposite of life. I am the distortion of birth. I am silence.

I long for daylight, for a remembrance of dawn. I see the sky covered in a thick purple hue more ominous than clouds of rain, a sky that has combined all the beauty and the evil of the world. It is a sky that claims two worlds.

I wait, in a purple sky.

My mouth threatens with a final drowning. The water moves, penetrates the darkness, pushes forward. A murmuring, a jarring motion, then a crash. I sink deep, beaten and helpless. My thought grows and grows into darkness, into night. I find my thought and my thought runs like a full and dirty stream on the side of a mountain not to be stopped but I follow my thought, wherever it goes, and my thought climbs trees, searches the bottom of rivers.

* * *

A snail moves blind beneath the green leaf and spreads a wet path over dying veins.

Father falls on my legs parted, spread on the cold floor.

He whispers, sings about a handful of sand gathered on the bank of rivers.

I cry for mercy, but my cry is silence. Mother, I cry in my sleep. A throbbing hard and horrid passes between my legs, searing, tearing. A wound fresh with blood grows into my chest. A seed grows on my navel, grows into a tree with firm roots that gather all the water from my stomach, pulls hard till my eyes are still, empty, and uprooted.

I fall from a tree, covered in thorns.

Father . . .

. . . blood in my crying.

He enters into me breathing hard. A snail spreads on stone, climbing upward, blind, pushing forward, its shell curled hard over its body, hiding from day in a deathly silence. The snail moves slow and searching over the rock, spreading through rock.

My stomach is hard like stone. I hear the sound of water breaking on rock.

In the darkness, he pulls hard at the roots of the tree, pulls at my navel. I cry between fierce fingers cradling my face . . . mother. A slow silent cry, futile.

I open my eyes.

Father . . .
Father . . .
Silence dark and still, vivid, like night sky.
Pushing. Pressing hard. He thrusts forward.
Father . . .

Night.
A hand dark and heavy descends over my face, over my eyes, tightens round my neck. My legs are crushed. My stomach is hard like rock.

He enters. I cry into the night but my cry returns to me and spreads down into my stomach like water, water, at the bottom of leaves, water, water beneath rock, water, water between my legs, water.

A snail moves over broken bones gathered on rock. A trail of saliva, of dew. My cry creeps from beneath rock.

Night.
My fingers are broken and crushed, white with bone.
Father . . .
My cry is death not life, softens, like stone breaking in water, softens, like saliva, softens, like rain.

I hear breathing, violent, breathing, on rock. A rigid silence.
Father . . . between my legs.

Wet between my legs. Blood wet wetness. Not flowing wet. Slippery. Not so loud.

He put mucus here, and blood . . .
Quiet.
He put mucus between my legs . . .
Quiet.
Am I going to die?
Quiet.
He broke my stomach . . .

He put blood between my legs.

The pain climbs upward through my chest. A searing cramping beneath my feet. An emptiness moves right through me, past me. A frantic cry, then silence. Rain falling into dream. I rise from my crying, trembling.

It is like this. He is breathing hard spreading a humid air around my face. A ringing awakening and something enters through my ears, ominous, and it will not depart. It spreads its darkness through me, past me, feigning friendship. The sound curls inside me like a leaf, and dries. He enters a dark breathing through my nose, thick with blood. He enters through my crying saying very softly sh sh sh. The earth sways underneath, ruptures, and I fall into the darkness. My hand seeks the darkness and finds a forehead grooved and moist, grooved and moist. He enters into me, through me.

A tearing screaming then he sings to me a lullaby about tiny fishes moving between reeds, and I must only think of them because they are lonely and afraid and so little and if I don't think of them they might never grow but only swirl always in the green deep of the water.

Zhizha

He calls, breathing into my sleep. A sound grows beneath my body, like breaking rock and bone.

Crush.

Darkness and blood. My eyelids pulse, throb, tear. A trembling swelling lower lip then darkness so complete; there is no sound, no footsteps, no thundering shout, no tomorrow. I am alone. A cough rises from my stomach, grows through me while a thin ray of light slices my eyelids. My forehead swirls. A flood of piercing light enters my eyes and I cry. I joy to hear the sound of my crying. I have woken up, survived. Maybe I will live.

. . . tell grandfather?

No.

. . . tell grandfather?

No. It is death when such things are told.

Grandmother . . .

It is night.

I feel my eyelids fall while my tongue grows thick and heavy, pressed between my teeth. My tongue is hard like stone. I dare not cry or breathe. A shadow grows towards me. Father grows out of the shadow. I wait beneath the shadow which pushes forward in a violent thrust, crushing my legs.

mucus and saliva . . .

enters . . .

It is night.

Blinding pain grows across my forehead, grows in my stomach, through me. My bones are broken and crushed. A cold hand presses hard on my knee, moves impatiently over my body, searching and digging. Fingers mumbling, muttering, cursing the darkness in a voice a husky quiet. A sudden shove, brutal and repeated. My knee breaks, slides sideways, contracts. My elbows are bruised and broken. He lifts my face, swings my head sideways, my head pressed down, my face cupped in his wide palm. Fingers enter into my eyes, mercilessly. He pushes sideways, sideways. He pushes at my broken knee. I cannot breathe. My forehead grows with a painful throbbing, grows into his waiting hand, grows into a rounded shell which he breaks and breaks with a clenched fist. I close my eyes and a black cloud spreads before the moon, like smoke.

A tortoise moves slowly forward, carrying a broken shell. It pulls its head inside, and hides. It pulls its legs in and hides. Its shell is broken and crushed because it has swallowed its own head, swallowed its own legs. Its stomach is hard like the earth, hard with the things it has swallowed. The neck twists and turns and swells slowly to one side. It totters slowly forward, wobbles on hidden legs, digs the ground slowly, frantically, burrows in the gathering earth. It hides, survives, moves slowly forward.

It is night.

Fingers reach and fold, thick with blood. I lie still. Then I hear my teeth fall from my mouth.
Father . . .

Father carries me in his hands, holds my head down with his fingers. Naked, I kick helplessly about. I cannot escape. I scrape the ground with weakening legs, with a dreadful torment, a feeble hope.
I open my mouth to fight or cry but my face is numb, dead. It has

been hammered with a rock.

Father . . .

A cry waits in my stomach.

My feet are heavy with water. Darkness, thrusting forward, darkness. I lie still and wait. My legs are heavy with the darkness, cold and dead. I shift desperately forward. My body moves, turns, twists backward. Something falls deep and down in the darkness. I crawl forward, move in water. I crawl forward. I creep, I sleep, slowly wake. I sleep. The darkness tightens around my forehead, presses me to the ground with a cruel hand, and I am swallowed by the ground which meets me in a stirring echo rising, a mingling of lament, a torment of grief.

It is morning. My voice grows from inside me, broken and dry, lies still, waits to be remembered, rises soft like smoke, creeps out of the room, calls for mother, wakes.

A word does not rot unless it is carried in the mouth for too long, under the tongue.

≈≈≈≈≈≈≈

# 24

1980 spelt the end of loneliness and unfulfilled desire long kept. There were those who had the mischance to hope, though hope was another name for losing; losing was not quick like death. It was slow and priceless, especially to those who had cried for the end of loneliness, who had turned loneliness into conviction. In many ways they were convicts of a belief which had told them that to be merely human was enough, and that waiting was reason enough to keep living. Few understood what maxims made living wholesome. Few bothered to understand. Few were not ensnared by dream. They were captives.

Where ceremonies were discovered and celebrated, in the city, it became commonplace to see women carrying mirrors into the middle of the streets and crashing them onto the tarred ground while a passing beaten car swerved and cursed and blew the horn. Rituals are born of adversity. Breaking mirrors in public places became a necessary ritual of abandon. Where mirrors could not be found empty bottles were broken to bring good fortune. There was something unfathomable in this easy act, courageous even. The sound and sight of breaking glass brought sharp edges to existence.

Breaking glass. Some said this was a ritual the women had invented in order to keep their longing ripe and ready for they missed their men, pressed their eyes together in sleep to lock out desire and lock in pain, their lips together too to muffle despair, bit into their tongues for a taste of tenderness long gone, cupped their hands to shelter a spilling futility, to gather a nameless comfort, somehow, and finally, even in sleep, especially in sleep, crossed their legs for good fortune. It was a time for rites of woe. They missed their men, the women. Missed them, missed them.

History had become dazed and circular. Usually a hand-sized mirror was broken with one swing of the arm, but once, a woman was seen dragging a mirror the size of herself into the middle of the street while a crowd of children followed. The story was carried from mouth to mouth till it returned to the mouth of the same woman who had performed the marvellous act. The story told how this woman lifted her arms and heaved the mirror into the air like one possessed and brought it down with a dazzling crash. History was a spectacle, and this woman had found a new dream to make her own waiting real, original to her suffering and her particular endurance of anguish. The path left strewn with dangerous glitter was fair warning to oncomers that caution made living an art. And when the broken mirrors had become forgotten there was only the hurt lingering underneath coaxing words, just hurt and living and waiting, lingering, not forgotten.

1980 was a time to shorten distances to desire. Even those who had been restless and unconvinced found it necessary to open their windows an inch wider, to raise their voices a tone just enough to be heard above the hopeful rhythm of those who had clung to the frayed edges of dream. These anxious few, who felt threatened by the progress of desires they knew little about, saw nothing of, found it necessary to search their pockets for an extra coin that would purchase opportunity, if nothing else; being poor was part of the loneliness that accompanied waiting. Their voices hewn, frail and listless, their longing almost forgotten – they had waited.

≈≈≈≈≈≈

≈≈≈≈≈≈≈

**Also by**
**Yvonne Vera**

Without a Name

Nehanda

Why Don't You Carve Other Animals

≈≈≈≈≈≈≈